]

THE RAVEN

A Preface

SETH ROGOFF

© 2017 by Seth Rogoff
Book design © 2017 by Sagging Meniscus Press

All Rights Reserved.

Printed in the United States of America.
Set in Adobe Garamond with LaTeX.

ISBN: 978-1-944697-44-0 (paperback)
ISBN: 978-1-944697-45-7 (ebook)
Library of Congress Control Number: 2017938425

Sagging Meniscus Press
web: http://www.saggingmeniscus.com/
email: info@saggingmeniscus.com

for Jana

FIRST, THE RAVEN

First, the Raven

A Preface

HO IS Jan Horak? A typical translator's preface—especially for a book by an author of this Olympian magnitude—might try to answer this question right away in the first few lines, at the very least in a concise page or two of biography, influences, and position in the literary canon. Eventually, I'll get to all that. At least I hope I'll get to it. I did intend to start with it, to start with what's essential for the reader to know, but one doesn't always get to the essential by traveling a straight path, and almost never can a translator depart from there. The essential bends and twists; it spirals off into the distance. Or it's there, but lost in the shadows, and if we're lucky a faint penumbra of essence glows behind the dark sphere. As I sit at my desk in Prague gazing out the window into the last rays of evening light, I feel compelled to begin the preface to my translation of Horak's *Blue, Red, Gray* in another place, a shadowy spot, on a cloud-covered night some weeks or months ago. I begin with an arrival.

I felt uneasy as I stepped from the taxi and gazed up through the twisted, leafless branches of an old elm and into the darkness. It was uneasiness like that of an unsettling dream, a strange sense that I wasn't who I thought I was, that I wasn't where I thought I'd be. The sign on the door in front of me said The Captain's Cabin and below it, in ocean-blue italics, *see you below deck!*

I made my way through this grimy back entrance to what was otherwise a fancy hotel and down a dimly lit, narrow staircase. I entered the bar, looked around, and took a deep breath to gather myself. The air smelled of old carpet and fried food. From a corner across the way, a large television set blared a stream of commentary to a live hockey game. The bar's furniture was nondescript, the décor shabby, dusty and oriented around a nautical theme, though only half-heartedly and cheaply pursued—

ships' wheels, model schooners, and maritime paintings. I couldn't help but consider the marble and brass cube around the bartender's pit as the very height of tastelessness and cringed at the thought that I had interrupted my work on the translation at its most delicate stage—the final stage—and come all the way from Prague to Portland to find myself in such a place. There was no good reason why Gabe would have insisted on meeting me here, especially given the many more suitable options for our reunion, even one provoked by those awful, awful circumstances—provoked, in other words, by the serious and apparently worsening condition of Gabe's wife, the dazzling Ida Fields.

Gabe sat by himself on a stool at the bar with a half-empty beer in front of him. Other patrons were scattered at tables, some in pairs, others in small groups, no more than a dozen in total. In addition, six guys sat in front of the television watching the hockey game. Even though I found hockey absurd and inexplicable, I would have rather joined their festive, manly society than to perch myself up on the stool next to Gabe. Added to the already disagreeable circumstances of our meeting was the fact that I was late. Not that it was my fault. The connecting flight in New York had left late and the baggage in Portland had taken forever to come. Thoughts of my travel—the early morning trip to the Prague airport by train and bus, the long flight, the interminable layover, and then the second flight to Portland—weighed on me, pressing me down into what might have been a blissful, cleansing sleep. I would have a single drink, I told myself, and then call it a night. This prelude would be over and the main scene, the reason for this trip, my meeting with Ida on the following day, would come. Instead of taking another taxi twenty or thirty minutes to my brother Henry's house, I considered getting a room upstairs in the hotel, even if the cost was beyond my budget, not that I would have admitted as much to Gabe, or even fully to myself. I'd been living outside the boundaries of my means for years, bailed out now and then by what always seemed like a single, miraculous (and quickly vanished) windfall.

Gabe watched as I approached with a blank look on his face. When I came nearer to him, he hesitantly rose to his feet to greet me. I saw immediately that he was slender, as he'd always been, and fit, which called to mind his stand-out high school cross-country and tennis careers. In general, Gabe looked good. He was freshly shaven, had neat brown hair, and his typical olive skin. At quick glance, it seemed as if Gabe hadn't aged a bit, like he was still the identical man I knew nearly twenty years ago. I wasn't expecting him to look this good, this vibrant and youthful.

From what Ida's letter had said, or at least implied, I had imagined I would encounter a lost and desperate being. And beneath that hale shell, that's what I believe he was, that's what he had to be.

He gestured to the stool next to his for me to take a seat.

"What're you drinking, Sy?"

"Whatever you're having looks good to me."

He waived to get the bartender's attention and then said, "Another one of these," pointing down into his glass. After taking a drink, he added, "How about making it two more?"

"Sure thing," the man said and pulled two glasses from the shelf.

By the time I had taken off my jacket and situated my suitcase behind the stool, my beer had arrived. I sat down next to my old friend.

"It's a peculiar place, an odd choice," I said when the bartender had moved away to attend to another customer. "How about finishing this round and going somewhere else for a bite to eat, somewhere with at least a window or two?"

"Just order something here," Gabe said matter-of-factly. "The burger is actually one of the best around. Besides, this is the only place I'll go these days."

"Why's that?"

"One reason is that I don't run into anyone here. It's mostly guests of the hotel. Mainly, though, it's because this is the only place in town where I don't get cell phone reception. Really, the only place, as if this bar is in some kind of digital vortex. It's an odd thing. Look," he said and held up his phone, "it just searches endlessly down here." He set it down on the bar. "And I can exist for a few hours in the serene void."

I shifted uncomfortably on my stool, trying to make something of the fact that Gabe was hiding out in this subterranean hole where nobody, including and especially Ida, could get in touch with him. I sensed he was trying to provoke me with such a statement, maybe to blame me for his fate. I wasn't going to take the bait. I had come back to Portland because I had been asked to come back. One could say, yes, one could say with confidence, that I'd been summoned back. Gabe, I guess, would have preferred if I had never come back and for him this was the worst possible way I could have returned. But what, after all, did he know about the manner in which I was returning? Nothing. Not a thing. I barely knew myself. It had been an excruciating fall and winter, nearly all of it spent with Jan Horak, trying to keep him sober for long enough to finish our work. It's a horrible role to be the man who takes on the responsibility to keep a drinker from drinking. And Horak hated me for it, I thought, as I picked up my glass of beer and took a sip. He hated me for pulling him out of those smoky Prague pubs. He hated me when I brought him home and forced him to drink black coffee and water or to eat a plain roll before going to sleep to try to prevent the usual vomiting. He hated when I would shout at him, "Enough!" humiliating him in front of his friends, or at least in front of the hangers-on or young enthusiasts who pretended to be his friends. But what Horak hated most was when I'd involve his wife Alena, from whom he had been long separated but on whom he was still quite dependent. When things with Horak got really bad, usually at the end of a protracted "wet" period, I would beg Alena to come to his magnificent but run-down apartment on Rieger Park and help get him back on his feet. In short, Horak was the bane and the beauty of my existence. His physical form tortured me. He abused me, at times even striking me in a violent burst of anger—and his anger at critical moments in our process could be monstrous. Far more importantly, Horak, and here I mean Horak's words on the page, delighted and inspired me. His writings as a dissident ranked with the best of the best. How could I capture the complexity of Horak, the totality of Horak, for Gabe, for this boy who sat beside me, now suddenly a man, who throughout his life refused to spread his wings and fly? It wasn't impossible to imagine, in fact it seemed quite likely, that despite what I knew from her letter, Ida had soared too far above him.

Gabe snatched his phone from the bar and slipped it back into his pocket.

"Ida doesn't mind that she can't reach you?"

He stared straight ahead for a moment and then said, "Are you kidding me, Sy?" He paused. I remained silent. "After all these years, you walk into this bar and that's what you're going to say to me? It's unbelievable—or actually, it's entirely predictable." He reached up and ran his hand through his hair. "If things weren't what they are, if Ida wasn't the way she is, I'd be out of here right now. As it is, I'm not sure why we're doing this, why the hell we're doing this."

"I was surprised to get her letter."

"And we yours. It was just about the last thing I was expecting to deal with. The only thing that could possibly top that letter is your actual appearance here."

"Did Ida tell you what she wrote to me? Did she say that my letter was a response?"

"Of course not," he said and took a long drink from his beer.

Of course not, I repeated to myself and shifted uncomfortably on the seat. The damn stool was hurting my back, especially after the long day of travel. I stood up and leaned against the brassy rail, stretching my body back and forth to relieve the pressure. As I did this, a loud noise erupted from the group of hockey fans, followed by a round of hand slapping and back patting. Horak, a huge hockey fan, had forced me to be present at dozens of viewings of the sport over the previous years. A good deal of my hatred of it, I have to confess, comes from these experiences. Whether events went for or against his favored team, Horak used the games as an excuse to drink excessively. God help us if the outcome were unfavorable! At those times, Horak's already explosive anger would transform into an infantile rage, often resulting in him being forcibly removed from whatever location he had chosen on that particular night. I was amazed at the intensity with which Horak watched these games, these "events" as he called them. He lived the game fully, as he lived much of life—and as he wrote. The fullness of his existence shocked and unsettled me at times, especially when I compared it to the seemingly spare nature of my own. If only, I often thought, Horak could focus as much attention on our common work as he did on professional ice hockey, we might have already finished! The idea that this great writer, this philosopher, one of the leading dissident voices in the Eastern Block, a man who helped bring down the USSR, a true artist, author of monumental works like the post-1968 *Rain, Rain,* a man whose pages traveled from hand to hand in dimly lit pubs, cafés, or were passed on the street by discreet switching of bags and briefcases, a man whose life's work culminated with the publication in 1989 of one of the century's greatest *samizdat* novels, *Blue, Red, Gray,* which was never (until now!) translated into English—that such a man, greater in my opinion than Pasternak or even Milosz, could sit enthralled by a game of ice hockey and react with the passion of a pre-teen boy (tantrums, tantrums!) never ceased to confound me.

"The situation with Ida is horrible," I said to Gabe, "I was shocked to hear it, shocked to hear about the whole thing."

"I'm not sure what you mean, Sy. Tell me how you see the whole thing? I'd really like to know. Maybe I came out tonight to find that out—to find out what you think this so-called whole thing is."

"The whole thing is Ida, isn't that clear enough? What else could it be but what's happened to Ida, to her nature, her being, her spirit? What I read in that letter, that isn't the Ida I knew."

"The Ida you knew? That's nothing but empty nostalgia—or something worse, much worse. The only thing that's clear to me is that you were ready to hop on a plane for Portland at a moment's notice."

What a statement! I held back and let Gabe's words hang over the bar. It seemed to me like he was playing a role better reserved for one of his lead characters. He had a way of forming such embattled heroes, heroes reeling from immediate or distant shocks—at times simply reverberations—ordinary people at once lovable and contemptible, but who at critical moments acted (or tried to act) with a truly generous heart. Gabe was a playwright and, I have to admit, a pretty decent one, at times a very good one, at others maddeningly pedestrian. It had been many years since he last sent me a script to read. That happened just months before the event veiled by his *hop on a plane* remark. It was Ida, not I, who had been ready to hop on a plane. She "hopped" on a plane to come to see me when I was still living in Berlin, living with Florian. Florian—it's hard even to write that name considering our current adversarial relationship. And yet Florian played a key role in my life. It was Florian, after all, who introduced me to Horak during a trip to Prague in December of 1996. I went along as a tourist while Florian and Horak spent ten intense days finishing off the German translation of *Rain*,

Rain and making plans to begin work in the new year on his magnum opus, *Blue, Red, Gray*. Our last evening in Prague found the three of us out at one of Horak's regular pubs, a dingy, smoky place below the Prague Castle. After some half dozen glasses of beer, a mere warm-up for Horak, Florian, quite drunk, began what amounted to a half-hour monologue on why I, Sy Kirschbaum, was the one and only choice as translator for the first-ever English edition of *Blue, Red, Gray*, this despite my complete ignorance of the formidable Czech language.

"No, no," I protested, "I couldn't possibly do it. Absolutely not." Strangely, the more I refused, the surer Horak was that I was the guy. He had already rejected three English translators over the past five or six years for various reasons, including one on the grounds that the guy (a Yale PhD) had what Horak called "communist-influenced Czech." He liked the notion that I would be learning the language purely for the book. His Czech, he declared, would become my Czech. If only such a thing were possible! In any case, a month later, both bewildered and youthfully cocksure, I found myself sitting in a new suit and pair of shoes in a New York office agreeing to the terms of the contract and signing a series of papers. Six months after that heady day in New York, I moved from Berlin to Prague to fully immerse myself in Czech and to prepare to deliver the massive work—massive both in terms of its length (well over 1,400 pages) and sagacity—to the English-speaking world. And these intervening months would have fallen into blurry oblivion had not Ida arrived abruptly in the middle of February. She stayed for three months—three horribly short months, or to put it another way, the only three months I have fully lived on this planet, maybe the only three months during which I have felt that my life is fully real.

We were twenty-three years old. Who would have thought that only now, seventeen years later, would I be approaching the end of a project agreed to in such a drunken haze, a haze of great enthusiasm, a haze produced by the radiant glow of Horak's colossal mind, a mind that it takes (even now at the age of sixty-seven) more than a dozen beers to knock back down to earth? One thousand, four hundred and fifty-six pages—well over half a million words. Well over. I've lost count of the precise number, and even my computer gave up the task of counting words already back in 2005. Finally, it's done. All that remains, per the 1997 agreement, is for Horak to finish initialing the pages of the English manuscript, marking it as approved and therefore as complete and ready for the final copy edit. Needless to say, given Horak's sensibility and his drinking, this process was dragging on and by the time I received Ida's summoning letter, three weeks before my meeting with Gabe, it had entered its second year.

Hop on a plane. This is what it seemed Ida had done after a major verbal brawl between her and Gabe—she would never say what the fight was actually about. Theirs was an affair that began during our third year of high school. To my surprise, Gabe announced that fall that he would be entering the state one-act play competition. He had spent the previous summer working on the script. The play had just one character, a seventeen-year-old girl, and three scenes. On that balmy September evening, as we walked through Portland's downtown on our way to our favorite coffee house, Gabe declared his intention to cast Ida Fields in the single, starring role. Not knowing how to respond to this piece of devastating news, I flipped a joint out of my jacket pocket and lit it up, taking a couple of puffs before handing it over to Gabe, who took it despite it being in the middle of his cross-country running season. Only on the most exceptional occasions would Gabe smoke pot during his running season, but the name "Ida" being passed between the lips of her two greatest admirers was certainly an exceptional occasion.

I met Ida in the eerily abandoned hall of the not-yet-totally-defunct Tempelhof Airport as she flew in from Brussels on a connecting flight. Young Ida Fields. It was her first trip abroad. I had been in Berlin for almost two years at that point. She looked even better than I remembered. She was magnificent, in fact, and at first sight, her entering that cavernous half-dead space, everything I had ever felt for her—my entire arsenal of desire—broke free of its shackles and filled my head with a type of euphoria I had never experienced before or since.

She walked up to me and said with a half-smile, "There you are." I had nothing to say in response. We embraced. She pulled me tight. I did the same. Hop on a plane! I did nothing but open my arms to an old and dear friend. She walked into them. She walked in! How on earth could I be blamed for that? She walked in!

As this memory of Ida lingered in my mind, a guy came up and stood next to me at the bar.

"Crazy night out there," he said, removing his jacket and scarf.

"Seems normal enough to me," I said.

"Not anymore, buddy. The snow's started. It's coming down and it's sticking. It's going to be a big-time storm." He flagged the bartender, put in an order and then joined his friends at a nearby table.

I turned back to Gabe, taking my seat again on the stool. Since I had arrived, more people had come in and now there was a real bustle in The Captain's Cabin. Gabe was looking across the room, his eyes focused on nothing in particular. I knew that distant look and it occurred to me at that moment that I still knew him, Gabe, even after all this time. I knew him, deeply, and if I knew him, it stood to reason that he also knew me and also deeply.

"Where are you living these days?" I asked, trying to relocate the encounter on a new bit of terrain.

"Over on the East End, close to the theater."

"And how's the theater?"

He turned and stared at me for a few moments, his eyes piercing into me as if to discover the hidden secret to the whole affair. Then he took a drink of his beer and said, "Alright, Sy, fine, let's do this. The theater? It's a god-damn slog most of the time. It's exhausting, especially now without Ida. I'm taking the year off to get back to writing. I haven't written a thing in years. But first things first, I have to figure out this situation with Ida. If it takes you coming all the way from Prague for it, if it necessitates us hanging out at a bar over a few beers, that's the way it has to be. And I have to deal with it. At least now, at least for tonight, I have to participate in whatever the hell this is. There's no script for us now, Sy, just an endless string of improvisation. Where the hell's the sense in that?"

"That's right," I said, "I remember now, you love when

16

things make sense, when everything adds up in the end. Coherence. But it doesn't work that way. Horak knows that better than anyone. This is precisely what makes him great, what makes him a towering figure. Horak would never ask a question like the one you just asked."

Gabe looked at me for a minute or two without saying anything. At some point a strange grin came to his face and then quickly vanished. "I need some fresh air," he said. "I'll be right back."

"Sure," I said as he stood up from the stool and wandered away from the bar toward the door through which I had entered not long before. When I turned back to my beer, I felt a distinct sense of tiredness. I propped my elbows up on the marble and set my chin down in my open hands. No sooner had I reached a blissful state of semi-consciousness then the bartender, who had in the meantime come over quite close to me, said, "A long day today?" The sound of him pouring small pretzels into a wooden bowl stationed between my beer and Gabe's completely shattered my peace.

"You could say that."

"How about another one of those?" he asked, pointing to my near-empty glass.

"Why not."

"Wonderful," he said for no discernible reason. The order of another beer seemed to me anything but a cause for celebration.

I thought about Gabe, Gabe Slatky. Gabe to me, then and forever, and not Gabriel, as Ida took to calling him during those rehearsals for the one-act play competition, which they won after Ida's final triumphal performance in March of that year. I never called him by his last name, Slatky, or by that horrid derivative, Slats. Just Gabe. Only Gabe. He was my Gabe, related only partially to Ida's Gabriel or to "Slatky" or "Slats." I've known Gabe for most of my life. We met in afternoon Hebrew school when we were in first grade. I was a skinny and exuberant kid, always in motion, always talking, always searching, he a tanned and sturdy introvert, an observer, a careful child. At the time, Gabe was going to the private school near his family's house in the West End while I attended the public elementary school in our neighborhood. The Slatky residence, a 1880s brick mansion built by the molasses magnate Cornelius Burnham, was an impressive and austere structure. Gabe's father, Jerry Slatky, had been a computer engineer. He had founded a small company in Boston, moved it to Portland in the late 1970s, and then sold out to IBM around 1981 or 1982, making what I can only imagine seemed to Mr. Slatky like enough money to last a lifetime. He used the cash to start a bunch of other ventures and to invest in this and that, but nothing else worked out. In fact, the whole process eventually led to financial disaster for the Slatky family, culminating in 1989 when the two Slatky kids were pulled out of the expensive Howell School and unceremoniously dropped into the public high school. Gabe and I, accordingly, entered high school as freshmen together. Even though we had known each other for eight years at that point, it was the first time we were proper schoolmates. From the first day of high school our friendship was transformed. We were practically inseparable.

Gabe was good looking, even as a boy. But his good looks didn't lead him, like so many similar specimens, to date prom queens and cheerleaders or to ruthlessly exploit the overwrought emotions of teenage girls in order to perform sexual conquest. Gabe, in fact, didn't date anyone until Ida. I partly suspect this is because he was in love with her (as I was) from the beginning, from that first day of that first year of high school when she appeared in those barren hallways wearing a tight yellow woolen dress and a purple scarf, seemingly having stepped directly from our wildest and most lurid imaginings into actual life.

As for Gabe's intellectual acumen, this is a bit more complicated. He wasn't an excellent student, primarily because it always took him a little longer than the best students (myself included) to grasp the material. Despite all this, despite his clear mediocrity in many ways, there was something about Gabe that was special—and it had nothing to do with the typical high school subjects. This quality swirled around the central force that animated his plays—his authentic and unshakable sense of humanity. This humanity gave Gabe the grounding to construct scenarios that brought the audience deep into the moral fog and then back out again. The result was not so much transformation but unease. Gabe was a master of producing a type of nervous fluttering in one's chest. For years, I had no idea Gabe had these talents, though looking back I can say that I always felt them there. Because I felt them, I trusted him. I trusted Gabe more than I trusted anyone, more than I have trusted anyone since our friendship loosened and then unraveled completely during those stormy winter days of 1997. Yes, it's safe to say that in his mind I betrayed him utterly. But what right did Gabe have over Ida? Had Ida no volition? I would think, given his incredible ability to parse the moral threads, he would have been able to see Ida's trip to Berlin for what it was, for whatever the hell it was!

Though he'd done short sketches here and there, the one-act with Ida was his first real shot at writing a play. The result was tremendous. I was stunned by the play's beauty, and I'm not just talking about Ida's perfect performance—or how she looked wearing that thin white robe and lit up at every possible angle by a luminous stage light that seemed to elevate her and cause her to float through the otherwise empty space. No, Gabe's work, his craft, was fantastic. I sat there in the audience during the premier and burned with admiration and jealousy. It seemed to me like he suddenly existed in a realm totally out of my reach. Gabe was now a star. Teachers started to defer to him. Girls turned their eyes his way. But none of this changed him. The big difference was that he had gotten together with Ida during the months of rehearsal. Our duo—Sy and Gabe—became a group of three, and as a part of this trio I got to know Ida Fields, to understand the unbelievable complexity of her being, its depth, its range. Or perhaps I didn't understand this at all—and how could I have understood this? I had no tools to understand Ida, no way of grasping the full scope of her spirit, itself partially eclipsed by her stunning, peculiar and unique beauty. Ida. Ida. Ida. In any case, beginning with that performance Ida would play a central role in my life, a role that would culminate in 1997 in Berlin—only to suddenly and unexpectedly reopen some weeks before my last trip to Maine. And why was I in Berlin? On the one hand, I was there to embrace a bohemian life. There were few alternatives to such an existence in Berlin in the 1990s. It was anarchic and ephemeral and yet as slow moving as the stillest river, the clearest sky. Nothing moved, nothing changed and at the same time everything changed at every moment—with a mere blink of the eye one's life in Berlin, my life, could transform, and the moment just before the blink, gone and unimaginable—inconceivable, irretrievable. In such a state, I drifted through that beaten-up cityscape with no love for it, but with a fascination for it, a need to be there. I wrote freelance. I translated texts from German to English. Through Florian, I received my first job, the *Forest Poems* of Ingrid Müller, luscious, verdant verse that pushed me to the edge of my capacity. But I grew from it. The poems forced me to work in new ways, to find radically different forms. Next came Daniella Kern's *Something Else to Say*, another collection of poetry—lyrical, sexual, and deviant. I finished it quickly after weeks of intensive, intimate sessions with the author. Then I got my first novel, Anton Grassfeld's *Trending Toward Zero*, a murky and confused work, which I would have abandoning half-finished if I didn't really need the money. Jobs continued to flow in and I learned how to immerse myself in a text, to exist in a world of another's creation, just as I learned how to surrender myself to the pulsating beat of the city, a city trembling, a city on the precipice of becoming, a city scarred and ugly, a city at once of history and without past, a city with only youth. On the other hand, I was not seeking Berlin but fleeing, fleeing Ida, fleeing Gabe.

My new beer arrived and I took a sip. Diagonal from me, a pair of fashionably dressed young women, one in pink, one in red, sat down and ordered cocktails. I looked over at them, wondering how old they were, where they were from, whether they were out for a single libation or whether this first drink was a stage-setting for a more adventurous, uninhibited evening, a snowy, blustery evening, an evening of recklessness, promise and danger.

As I was indulging in this bit of staring, Gabe returned and sat back down. "Henry always tells me a bit when I run into him," he said and positioned himself on the stool, "but you can imagine Henry's version. I'd like to hear directly from you about what's going on in Prague." He seemed to be in a less confrontational mood, at least the anger or animosity or hatred in his eyes had faded. Maybe he sensed, as I sensed, as I knew, as he knew, that it was the only way forward to her, to Ida.

"You don't need to ask me questions out of politeness. For god's sake, wherever we are, we're beyond that."

"Come on, Sy, what about it? The book, the translation?"

23

"You mean the Horak?"

"I guess, yes, the Horak."

"The book seems like nothing but an extension of Jan Horak the man at this point. I can't seem to separate the two."

"Who's the man?"

"Horak, the man. Let's see," I started and tried to find an entry point into the colossus of Jan Horak. His form, his shadow, towers above me day and night, in waking life and in dream, and yes, I dream of Horak, often terrible dreams, dreams which approach nightmare but then bend into something else, as Horak, or the idea of Horak, bends into a curve with a trajectory toward the infinite. "He's hard to describe, hard to capture. For one, he's got two kids, both grown up now, Milan and Anna. He almost never sees them. In the seventeen years I've been working with Horak, I've met Milan only twice and I don't think Horak sees him more than a couple of times a year. He's a photographer, but Horak says he's not a very good one—doesn't have the eye, or something like that. And Horak would know good work. In addition to being a writer, Horak's also a great painter, or was a great painter. He hardly paints now after a tremor developed in his right hand, his painting and writing hand. It's similar with Anna, but nowhere near as extreme. There's the typical father worship on her part and a particular type of doting on his."

"How old is she?"

"Early forties, a couple of years older than we are. They had her young. Horak was twenty when they had her, twenty-two or twenty-three when Milan came. Dates are important to Horak, as if some gnostic meaning can be derived from the fact that he was born in 1948, the year the Czech government fell into the Soviet sphere, and Anna in August 1968, exactly during the end of the Prague Spring. In fact, Horak's *Rain, Rain* is mostly about the birth of a child as the Soviet tanks roll through Prague. It's hard for me to believe I've known Anna for so long. She was a student at the university when I met her. She was studying American literature, focusing on Norman Mailer of all people. Maybe Mailer reminded her of her father, of Horak, though the two are completely different. But both are a certain type of man, a man who'll drink till sunrise and then grab a pen and just start writing, a man who knows how to engage, to fight and struggle. Boxers—though of course Horak would never actually box. I don't know. I don't know anything about Mailer, even though in the first years in Prague I'd help Anna out with her work from time to time. Now that I think about those days, Anna used to call her father Norman as a joke. I think she saw

25

something in Mailer's ferocity that she liked. But Mailer didn't have Horak's style, his beauty or grace. Not to say Horak is too polished. Far from it. He's gritty and graceful at the same time. In Czech that is. It's hard work getting it just right in English."

"Anna sounds interesting," Gabe said and took a drink. He wasn't looking at me but away at the other side of the bar, perhaps at the women in pink and red. I could tell he was having a hard time looking at me, seeing me.

"Interesting, for sure," I said, "but getting involved with Anna, if that's what you're implying, would've been suicide. Horak was enough to deal with. If I'd added more into the mix, I don't think I would've made it. And I barely made it—am barely making it out of there! Out of the Horakian universe. Besides, I was with a Canadian woman around that time, Meg, but it never developed into a long-term thing. She was in the city for a couple of years to do research on dissident writers and I set up some meetings with Horak for her. As usual, Horak gave her nothing but cryptic and impenetrable responses, which she then brought to me for a sort of exegesis. She got what she wanted, or what she thought she wanted, and then took off. It's nothing worth talking about. I liked her, Meg, that is, and maybe even Anna in some vague way. Or maybe in a more specific way." I stopped and took a drink.

"And now you're back here. For how long?"

"For however long I'm needed."

"But you're not needed, Sy. There's nothing to be done. There's nothing for you to do."

"That's not what Ida's letter said. I thought you would've read it. I was sure Ida would've shared it with you. I assumed that's why you called."

"No. Not at all."

"Maybe it's connected with Ida leaving the theater. That means something, that's something big after all these years—all these years since that first performance, since your first play together."

Gabe took another drink. "The theater is just part of a much larger canvas," he said, "but I can't see it. I'm too close to it. It's fuzzy, out of focus."

"Then step back from it. Take a step back. Maybe that's all that's required."

"Don't you get it, Sy? Ida would vanish if I step back. You wouldn't believe how much she's sleeping—or not sleeping but lying in the bed in the guestroom in some sort of in-between state. Some days she barely gets up. She didn't leave the theater in any active sense. She faded away from it. We created a theater here. We did it, Ida even more than me. Ida's the visionary. She's the force. She's the beauty. On some level, it's like her psyche collapsed.

And suddenly here you are, Sy. No. I doubt it. I doubt that's really it. I don't accept that."

Before I had a chance to say anything, Gabe and I were flanked by the group of hockey fans, who had migrated to the bar during a break in the action. They were talking loudly with each other about the game and calling out to the bartender for a round of drinks. Even after their beers were ordered, they stood crowding us, reaching by us to access the bowl of pretzels recently re-filled and then crunching the pretzels in our ears. Four of the six then shouted out orders for a burger and fries, while the other two agreed to head outside for a smoke.

"Not watching the game?" It was a man in his mid-forties.

"Not tonight," I said.

"You're missing a battle. The B's are up one after one."

"Definitely a slug-fest," another guy said as he leaned over the bar to Gabe's left, "as always with the Sabres."

The beers arrived and the remaining non-smokers grabbed them from the counter.

"You two in town for business?" asked the first guy.

"I live here," said Gabe.

"And what about you?"

"I'm over in Europe," I told him, "but I'm from here, I grew up here."

"Europe. No shit. I've been across the pond a few times. Wife and I spent our honeymoon in Paris. Went back to Tuscany a few years ago—incredible. Whereabouts are you?"

"Prague."

"That Poland?"

"Czech Republic."

"Right. Czechoslovakia. Must be interesting. You there for work?"

"In a manner of speaking," I said, "I mean, I'm working, but I wouldn't necessarily say I'm there for work. I guess I'm just there. Just there to be there."

"Got it, I understand that. Hell, I'm just here, too," he said and laughed. "Hey fellas," he called out to the others, "we've got a philosopher in the bar tonight. He's just 'there to be there.' That's a good one. I'll tell that to my wife when I stumble in tonight after the game. I was just at the bar to be at the bar. Brilliant. Name's Jim by the way, Jim Morgan. Over there we have Eddie Cox, Charlie Baxter and Bob Nichols. The two fools out in the snow are Carl Tasker and Mikey Halls."

I scanned them absentmindedly at first, still thinking about how I would pick up with Gabe—with his frustrating *I doubt that's really it* assertion. At first glance, they seemed like an anonymous pack of middle-aged locals.

29

As I started focusing a little more, though, and imagining their guts shrunken back into their abdomens, the puffy cheeks receding into more angular cheekbones, the gray hairs turning back to lush browns and blacks, thinning here, thickening there, fingers and arms leaner, slacks replaced by jeans, wingtips and loafers by sneakers, the group began to achieve a deeper familiarity, a past, a connection, however loose, to my past. It occurred to me, and also I'm sure to Gabe, that we knew some of these guys, at least indirectly. Carl Tasker, one of the smokers, must have been related to Tanya Tasker, a sweet, bookish girl a year behind us in high school. Bob Nichols had been a standout football player in his high school days. And Eddie Cox was the older brother of Dan Cox, a classmate and something of a friend of ours, who disappeared for months during our senior year to undergo intensive therapy and rehabilitation to overcome a heroin addiction. God knows what happened to him—a poor, insecure, and lonely kid. Even Morgan was somehow familiar.

"And you two gentlemen?"

"I'm Gabe Slatky and this is Sy Kirschbaum."

"Kirschbaum? You must be related to Henry Kirschbaum. We went to high school together. You his little brother?"

"That's right."

"Haven't run into Henry in quite some time, great guy though, one of kind. Real decent hockey player, too."

"I guess so."

"You married, Kirschbaum?"

"No."

"Well, don't worry about it. You've got time. It'll happen. I married a girl I met just before college ended. Moved back from Boston when Jenny got pregnant. We wanted to raise the family here, like your brother. And here you are, Henry Kischbaum's little brother, traveling the world. Man, it must be nice to have that freedom. Not that I could handle it. But I could manage for a few weeks here and there. Until then, I always have this place, right Chuck?" Jim shouted out to the bartender and symbolically raised his glass.

"I'm sure you're right, as always," Chuck shouted back. I was perplexed and annoyed by this theater.

"It's a great place to watch a game. No nonsense down here. No distractions, just the game, beer, and the boys."

Cox announced that the second period was about to start and the group moved slowly back toward the glow and hum of the television. "Tell your brother old Jimmy Morgan sends his regards. When you see him, you can give him my card." He handed me a business card of a company

31

called Maxwell and Morgan Financial. I slipped it into my jacket pocket.

"I'll be sure to pass on the message."

In the meantime, the two smokers had returned. "It's a real storm out there," one of them said, brushing the powder from his shoulders. "Roads are already a mess."

"Not much changes here," said Gabe when we were left alone again.

"The past is suffocating," I replied, more out of habit than deep conviction.

"Can't be any different in Prague or anywhere else for that matter."

"But it's not my past, it's not so personal."

"The personal's all we've got," Gabe said, finishing his beer and waving to Chuck for another. "It's ugly and boring and horrific at times, but it's also the only thing that's real. This is it, Sy, this is all there is."

"When does Ida expect you home?"

"She doesn't expect me. She doesn't expect anything anymore. At best, she'll notice, but more likely she'll be in the guestroom and won't give a damn."

"I should get going. Henry's waiting." Gabe looked worried when I said this—and in truth I said it at least in part to see how he would look. I had no intention of going anywhere at that moment, though I'm not sure why I felt compelled to stay. And that I needed to stay was totally clear—likely to both of us—just as it was clear that Gabe, too, needed to stay. "We can have another round in the meantime," I said and signaled to Chuck to make it two more.

The manuscript of *Blue, Red, Gray* is piled high on my desk as I write this account of my time with Gabe. It's nearing midnight. I sat down determined to begin my (unauthorized) note on the translation, which I have no choice now but to publish separately from the novel. Beside my notebook, the novel's fourteen hundred and fifty-six pages rise resolutely toward the high ceiling, or heaven, or simply into thin air. Tomorrow, I'm scheduled to meet with Horak at his apartment for what should be our last session on the book. Twenty pages remain for this final proof—twenty pages, which have been shuffled this way and that countless times. Now they await his scrawled initials, his stamp, his verification that I have read the words aloud to him and he has agreed. There's no telling how long it might take. Twenty pages can be an hour, a day, or even a week. I can only hope that Horak remains calm tonight, that some inner impulse to finish the project drives him earlier than usual from one of his favorite pubs and into bed. I have already procured the box for the manuscript. The publisher knows how close we are. The original acquisitions editor, Carl Glaser, remains at the publishing house, though by now he has been thrice promoted. Carl, the Chief as I call him, has stood by patiently, perhaps too patiently, and allowed the "process" to run its course. A book of this magnitude, this length, this importance to the historical and literary record, the Chief has told me many times—both on my desperate calls to the office and on his swings through Prague amid one of his literary tours—is no mere "novel" but rather a world within a world, part of humanity's collective consciousness. By the end of to-morrow, I might be done! Free of it! Empty of it, and thus empty of so much more. The prospect is unsettling, even terrifying.

I'd been avoiding the topic of Ida and Gabe's daughter Hannah, as it seemed Gabe had, but now I felt compelled to bring her up. I'd never met her and knew practically nothing about her, except that she was around six or seven years old.

"And Hannah?"

He twitched. He ran his hands through his hair, folded down the cuffs of his shirt. He closed his eyes and pressed his lids down hard. Without opening them, he said, "It's really hard on her. She needs Ida. Needs her in every way. And she's just not getting it. It's hard to watch. Actually, it's goddamn torture to watch. I can barely stand seeing her go to Ida only to see Ida do what she does—or what she doesn't do. And I hate Ida for it. I never thought I could really hate her, even when she came back from Berlin I didn't hate her." He turned to me. "I didn't hate you either, Sy. It wasn't hate. It was something much bigger and more complicated than hate with you and also with Ida. Ida got it. She understood. You just ran from it, avoided it. You bolted. Anyway, the sad thing is that otherwise Hannah couldn't be better. She's adorable, Sy, full of life. She needs me with her a lot now. And I need her. She's a touchstone, a grounding force."

"I can't believe I've never met her, never seen her. Not even a picture."

"I've got a couple pictures on my phone," Gabe said and pulled the device out of his pocket for the second time. He fingered at it for a few moments and then handed it to me.

I felt a strange rush of nervousness as I gazed down at the first picture. A girl emerged in front of me. She had the same long, narrow face with the same sharp nose as her father. On some level, it was like looking down at a photograph of Gabe from the time when we first met, as if no time had passed between that day and this night, as if I were still six and he still six, as if we'd never grown up and nothing either beautiful or horrible had happened in his life or mine. Hannah's thin, silky blonde hair hung to her shoulders. She had it pulled off her face and fastened to the side with a silver clip, which caught the gleam of an off-camera light source, producing a burstlet of fire. She sat in an antique wing chair, precisely the type of furnishing that fit perfectly in the old Slatky molasses mansion in the West End. Hannah—long, silky blonde hair. It was of Ida's type though lighter in color. Ida's hair, Gabe's facial structure, out of which radiated Ida's eyes. Those eyes, which I had studied in excruciating, exhausting detail since I was fifteen until that winter of 1997, peered out at me from Gabe's phone and almost knocked me off that stool. Hannah's eyes contained that same sea of green surrounding the darkest possible shade of blue. The darkness of the blue could easily have been mistaken for ordinary blackness if the looker didn't really inspect the color, focus on it, immerse oneself in it so as to lose perspective of color altogether, to find that thinnest line between blue and black, that incredibly diaphanous and yet impermeable membrane that separated one tint or shade from the next. The hair, Ida's hair. The face, Gabe's shape. Those Ida-eyes, those perfect eyes. And Hannah's mouth, curled ever so slightly into the first haunting gestures of a smile— half Gabe, half Ida. Her arms, long and slender, reached their way toward the end of the chair's armrests, her fingers splayed out on the wooden curvatures. Her legs, stocking-clad, shot out in front of her and dangled in the air. Her skin seemed to have her father's olive complexion rather than her mother's paleness.

I slid to the next photograph. Hannah was wearing the same purple dress with the embroidery around the cuffs and collar. She had on the same light violet stockings. She stood at the edge of a Persian carpet, candles burned in the background on a small side table set next to a loaf of round challah bread, already half consumed. It was Rosh Hashanah. Hannah was at her grandparents' house for an evening of festivities. Her thin, delicate frame seemed fragile in this context, or perhaps I simply imagined the fragility of this small girl who was celebrating without her mother, who lay sick in bed back home. And perhaps this girlish fragility was also magnified by those regal furnishings, which once decorated the molasses mansion and now filled this modest cape on this very ordinary street in the middle of the most ordinary neighborhood imaginable, a house built in such a plain style that often as a high schooler I would walk right by it, lost in thought, only to ring the bell of a nearly identical cape a few houses down toward the bay.

I handed Gabe back his phone. *Ran away, avoided, bolted*, he didn't know the half it, which is to say that he knew precisely nothing. It was a fiction he created to deal with trauma, a fiction that concealed his role and his responsibility in the entire affair. Somehow, I couldn't keep looking at those pictures. If someone told me at that moment that a plane was about to leave from Portland to Prague, I would have leapt up immediately and spent every last cent I had on the ticket (admittedly, this would not have been enough).

"It's hard to imagine being depressed with a little girl like that around."

"It's a contradiction of the worst kind. I live in a perpetual contradiction. But I'd rather stay here forever if the only other option is to let her go."

"Is that true?"

"I don't know." He paused, took a deep breath and drank some beer. "It's strange that I've never made another friend like you, Sy. There was something elemental there. A person can't get rid of a thing like that, whether one wants to or not."

I was steadying myself to respond when I was suddenly captivated by a woman who entered the bar from the stairwell that led up to the lobby, traversed the moldering, green carpet and sat down two barstools away from Gabe. I peered around him as she caught Chuck the bartender's eye and ordered a vodka and tonic. As Chuck set about mixing the drink, she reached into her handbag and took out a paperback book. She opened it and slid out a red bookmark, which she placed on the bar to her right. I craned my neck to try to catch glimpse of the book's title, but the dim light and the angle at which she grasped the volume prevented me from seeing.

Gabe turned and looked in the woman's direction. "It's a strange thing," he said, "this habit of sitting here surrounded by a bunch of strangers, being both observer and observed, observed, that is, doing basically nothing. And this is the great social gathering point, the barroom."

"I wouldn't describe this place as great in any sense. There's practically no observation happening, except maybe Morgan's group sitting around the television in the back. But that's just mindless looking. Why on earth anyone would choose to come down here is beyond me, except, I guess, to wallow in self-pity or because a person gets trapped in the hotel by the snow."

"There's no pitying going on," he said, "the one thing, the vital thing, this place offers is a vantage point."

"Every place offers that and most others are far more interesting, far more beneficial for taking action."

"The less there is out there, the more there is in here. Inside. Inside one's self."

"That's an excuse for standing still, for going nowhere."

"Or a reason to stay put, a damn good one."

"Well, I have a good reason to get off this stool. I need to use the bathroom."

As I moved from the stool and crossed behind Gabe, I shot another look over at the woman reading the book. Just as I did, she lifted her eyes and they met mine. In all likelihood, I allowed my gaze to rest on her for a bit too long. I indulged it too much and the connection severed when she turned back down to her page. The abrupt severing of our exchange, though completely expected, meant that I, too, felt compelled to look away, denying me a chance to conduct a more detailed examination of her form. Now that was a vantage point worthy of the name, I thought as I moved by the hockey-watching crowd on the way to the men's room, feeling the first mild sensations of drunkenness. I distinctly remember having the thought at that precise moment that I should really just finish my beer and head up to Henry's place before the snow got too heavy, before I drank too much, before things with Gabe took a nasty turn.

I used the bathroom and moved to the sink to wash my hands. It disturbed me to realize that the sink top was made of the same cut of marble as the bar and that the faucets and fixtures in the bathroom matched the bar's brassy rail. Horrible, I thought, horrible. I approached the left-most sink and stared into the long mirror above it as the warm water soaked my hands. There I was, looking rather awful. The collar of my white shirt, erupting out of my light blue button-up sweater, was way off kilter, making me appear asymmetrical and disheveled. I tried to yank the collar back into position, but it refused to settle in the right place. Every time I had it just so, it would immediately tilt to the left. I splashed some water onto my face and tried to fix my hair. It didn't help that days before my trip I'd erred in entering a third-rate (to say the least!) Prague "salon" and received what must have been the most disastrous haircut of my life. My attempts to fix the most serious problems at home with a pair of scissors only made matters worse.

I looked at my reflection as if gazing at some apparition. I felt comically out of place in this bathroom, in this bar, in this city and country, even though I suspect (and suspected at the time) that this feeling had little in the way of reality about it. The fact was, I was in that bar, in that city and country—and I was most certainly in that bathroom, wearing that collared shirt underneath that light blue sweater. Much more likely, I thought as I stared at the beads of water clinging to the underside of my chin, was that my selfhood in Prague, my selfhood for the past seventeen years, that this had been the spectral one. I splashed more water on my face. Yes, I thought, my hair was lighter than Gabe's, my eyes blue to his caramel brown, my wan skin to his olive. I was shorter, a bit thinner, less perfect, less handsome. After they first got together, I couldn't shake the idea that Gabe had won Ida (won out over me, that is) based on looks alone. It scared hell out of me when I realized I was totally wrong.

As I wiped my face with a paper towel and yanked my sweater and pants back into decent form, I thought of Horak, or more precisely of Horak's looks. When I first met him as a man of around fifty, he was a mix of robustness and unhealthiness. The heavy drinking had already started to take a toll on his body, coloring and shape, to say nothing about his general temperament. Make no mistake, Horak was still youthful. His rich, dark hair was graying, but was full, allowing Horak to wear it on the longer side, as he had throughout the 1960s and 1970s as a youth and a young man. He was relatively thin back then, gave off the impression of lankiness, probably because he had a rather long, thin neck and dangly arms. His skin was not a healthy color, partly because of the drinking and partly because he almost never ate a fresh vegetable. Horak survived on meat, combined with either Czech dumplings or boiled potatoes. He also ate sporadically and was not the type to break off at a proper mealtime. During a longer work session of eight to ten hours, he might once or twice cut himself a slice of bread and smear it with butter or fat, preferably of the duck or goose. Otherwise, he'd just open a bottle of beer and sip it in silence as he gazed out his window at the park below his apartment. How he managed to acquire and retain such an apartment, despite his near criminal status with the authorities after the banning of *Rain, Rain*, is something I've never understood.

I left the bathroom and was pleased to see that the Reader was still on her stool—and still reading.

"Are you alright?" Gabe asked as I remounted. "You look pale."

"I'm fine," I said not wanting to let on that I was actually very tired and had frayed nerves. It was starting to really bother me that I still hadn't learned much about Ida's situation and that I had made no definite plans to see her, which was the whole purpose of my trip.

"When I saw Henry, he told me that you're almost done with the book. This thing might go down as a legend. It's got to be the longest translation project in human history. It must be such a wild thing to do."

"Wild to say the least," I said and realized that more than anything I wanted—needed—to tell my old friend Gabe about the book. I took a long drink from my beer, bringing the level down close to the bottom. Chuck, seemingly aware of the levels of all drinks around him, gestured to me to ask if I wanted another round. At that moment, despite everything, I felt some of the old openness return that had existed between me and Gabe, though whether or not it was there on Gabe's side I have no way of knowing. It occurred to me that during the long years of work on *Blue, Red, Gray*, I'd barely talked about the project with anyone—or more accurately, I'd talked endlessly about the project without saying much of anything about the book, the work of art, a work that set down a firm cornerstone in the otherwise airy structure of my existence. Twenty more pages! As I sit at my desk—this torture chamber—the minutes and hours creep toward morning. The meeting time with Horak is set for 10am. "Tomorrow," I told him earlier this afternoon in a voice somewhere between Henry V at Agincourt and high school basketball coach, "we finish!" I graze my fingers over the top page of the one thousand four hundred and thirty-six completed pages. The unfinished stack of twenty, a hillock, bound with a black clip, sits beside the mountain.

Just as I was working to conceive of a strategy to describe Horak's magnum opus to Gabe, a voice behind us rang out, "Hey there." We shifted on our stools and saw that a young woman, who had been talking to an equally young guy at the bar, had disentangled herself from her conversation and was standing near us, beer in hand. "I'm sorry to interrupt," she said. I glanced over and saw that her friend was staring down into his drink in a seeming attempt to avoid any culpability for her actions.

"No problem at all," Gabe said and rose to his feet. "Gabe Slatky," he announced as he proffered her his hand. I looked on as she took it, unsettled that he had so quickly and thoroughly divulged his name.

"I'm Elsie. And I already know who you are. I was at the talk you gave in the fall at Bowdoin, the O'Neill talk from the Playwrights on Playwrights series. It was incredible."

"Thank you for saying so," Gabe said and bowed his head a bit. His handsomeness and smoothness could be galling to the less endowed.

"I'm studying theater and acting with Ginny. I'm in her advanced playwriting course." Out of the corner of my eye I saw her companion dig into his jacket pocket, retrieve a pack of cigarettes and set it on the bar in front of him. Then he got up, slipped on his hat, grabbed the cigarettes and made for the staircase that led outside. His jacket remained on the back of his seat, marking his small bit of squatted territory.

"I've heard rumors," Elsie continued, "that you're going to give a two-week workshop for Ginny's students in the fall."

"Probably," Gabe said, "but it's going to be a small group. I told Ginny I can't manage more than that."

"I sure hope I can make it into that small group."

"And what about your friend out in the snow," I cut in, "is he also a theater guy?"

"You mean Paul? No, he finds theater too bourgeois or something."

"Where are you from, Elsie, if you don't mind me asking?" I continued, though in truth I was trying to figure out how to use this occasion to introduce myself to the Reader nearby.

"New York, just outside the city," she said, "but my father went to Bowdoin back in the 70s. He's originally from Maine."

"A legacy," I said and slid down from my stool. "It's good to keep some family traditions going, I guess, especially recently invented ones."

"This is Sy Kirschbaum. He's just flown in from Prague."

"Are you also a playwright?"

"Sy's a translator," Gabe said. "He's working on a novel."

"Which novel?"

"It's called *Blue, Red, Gray* by Jan Horak," I said. "He's a Czech writer. Maybe you've heard of his book *Rain, Rain.*"

"Never heard of it. What was the name again?"

"Horak. Jan."

"Sorry."

"It doesn't matter. *Rain, Rain* came out a long time ago and the English translation can't be described as stellar. The book never got the recognition it deserved. You'll definitely hear about the next one. *Blue, Red, Gray* is Horak's major work, his life's work, his masterpiece."

"Is he dead?"

"He's very, very much alive!" I said with a feeling of proud defiance. A dead Horak seemed to me at that moment utterly impossible.

It was at this point that the Reader turned to us and said, "I've read *Rain, Rain.* Twice."

As if an exclamation point, the moment the word "twice" left her lips the band of hockey fans, now accompanied by a few others, burst into shrieks of joy. The uproar was so thunderous that it drowned out the next thing the Reader said. It didn't help that one of the fans shouted at least twice, "Hey, Chuck, you gotta come see this replay," over the general din. The sudden outburst of noise, how-

47

ever, provided a convenient reason for me to extricate myself from conversation with Gabe and Elsie and to move over to talk to the Reader.

"Sorry," I said as I approached her stool, "I missed the last thing you said."

"I said it's one of my favorite books, despite what you say about the translation. I actually thought the translation was excellent, not that I know the original."

"What brings you down here? Not an ideal spot for reading."

"I'm in town for a job interview. I'm staying upstairs and needed to get out of the room for a while. I couldn't stand being in there pacing all evening."

"What's the job?"

"It's for a position in the English department at the university. American literature."

For a second, possibly longer, this piece of news stilled the expression on my face. My father had been the doyen of American literature at the local branch of the state university for the previous thirty years. About a year ago, he'd had something of a breakdown and was pushed into retirement. It's hard to say exactly what this breakdown was and why it happened when it did. The truth is that it seemed inevitable when it occurred, like it'd been coming for years, perhaps forever, and at the same time it was as if it would never actually arrive, this "breakdown," this break, this rupture, which caused my mother—a true hater of technology—to participate in a three-way video chat with me and Henry in order to make sense of it. The call was a disaster—needless to say nerves were frayed on all sides, though in truth there were only two sides, their side and mine. After that video chat, I didn't speak to my mother for a good six months or Henry until I called him to let him know I was on my way to Maine to meet Gabe, then Ida.

"May I ask your name?"

"Claire."

"I'm Sy. It's nice to meet you." She nodded and ran her fingers along the edge of her book as if stroking a kitten or small child. "I imagine you've got a busy day tomorrow."

"Busy, yes, but to tell you the truth, I'm not optimistic about my chances."

"Why do you say that?"

"Mostly because I know the other two candidates. Let's just say I'm the underdog. Not to mention that the whole process is most likely pointless—rumor is that the university is about to freeze all new hires, or all non-essential new hires, and nothing could be less essential these days than American lit."

"My father taught American literature for thirty years."

"What's his name?"

"Walter Kirschbaum."

"I know him! We were on a conference panel together in Chicago a couple years ago. He's great. Really funny."

"You mean he made a fool of himself."

"Nothing like that. He was actually very sharp."

"He hasn't been right these past years," I said, becoming keenly aware that this woman named Claire, having spent a day or two at a conference in Chicago with my father some years ago, probably had more insight into his condition than I had, his neglectful and distant son. It had been at least five years since I'd seen him.

"I heard about that."

"What did you hear?"

Claire told the story just like I'd heard it from my mother and Henry, without, of course, some key details—and with none of the details that involved me. One day early last spring, my father, for reasons unknown to the world beyond the family (and only partially to us), locked himself in his office and started to send emails of various odd sorts to people around the university, ranging from students to the university president. After some days, the emails stopped coming. For a day or two, nobody heard from him and there wasn't any noise coming from his locked office. Eventually, the dean of faculty called my mother, who informed her, incorrectly, that Walter, my father, had taken off abruptly for their condominium in West Palm Beach after unleashing his flood of text. He'd lied to her about his whereabouts, of course. Noises started coming from the office again, leaving no choice but to force the door. When they did, they—the head of campus security, a pair of local police officers, two medics, the chair of the English department and the departmental secretary—found my father in his underpants and a tank top, office heated to around ninety degrees. He was sitting in front of an old typewriter with a page loaded in and typed to the bottom. The page had just one sentence, repeated over and over again. It read: *If I'm out of my mind, it's all right with me.*

"Those are the basics," I said, "at least the ones that circulated." I had no desire to fill in the gaps.

"What happened to him after that?"

"He was pushed out. No dignity in the end. Maybe it's the way he prefers it—it fits with his general Bellowesque view of things. The great collapse of dignity, or the persistence of dignity in the face of the collapse of dignity, which leads to a higher form of dignity. He might call it the 'dialectic of dignity,' something he could imagine coming from the mouth or pen of Moses Herzog. Maybe his conference paper in Chicago talked about it, predicted his own collapse, saw it in the text, read it between the lines. No one can claim that my father isn't a talented reader. He reads whole books, whole existences between the lines of books. For him, there's always an invisible book within a great work of literature, at least one, maybe more, maybe a dozen. But he's also ecstatic, uncontrolled and undisciplined. The pieces never fit together. The argument never thrusts forward. He could evoke, but he couldn't thrust. He could conjure, but he couldn't prove. Yet he wanted nothing more than to thrust and to prove."

"Whatever actually happened," Claire said, "I'm sorry about it. He's such a kind man. I never really believed the gossip."

I felt moved, almost joyous, by her doubt of the official record. "Yes, he's kind, too kind to fight. He just let himself be pushed out, walked calmly down the hall from his office to the door as the departmental secretary prodded him from behind with a sharpened no. 2 pencil."

"It seems like he wasn't in much condition to fight."

"What would he be fighting for anyway? For another year jammed into his pathetic office with its cinderblock walls? He should have quit years ago. He should've gotten on to something else. But that was totally incomprehensible to him. Something else—there was nothing else—nothing outside of that cube, nothing beyond those walls." Claire finished her drink and set the glass down on the bar. "Can I get your next round? You're welcome to join me and my friend Gabe." As I said this, I looked behind me and saw that Gabe was still talking with Elsie. Paul, her friend, was nowhere in sight.

"Maybe just one. I don't want to show up to the interview with a hangover. What would your father think if he heard?"

"He'd think you'd done it completely wrong and at the same time exactly right," I said, imitating for a moment my father's extravagant and muddled way. Then I called out, "Hey, Chuck, can you fix her another one of these?"

The bartender responded with his typical curt nod and his well-worn "sure thing."

"Let's move to a table," I suggested and called over to Gabe to let him know I was abandoning my berth at the bar. His face indicated concern at the decision, but he didn't say anything against it. After a couple of minutes, he pulled up the chair next to me. Elsie followed.

"What do you think happened to Paul?" I asked as she sat down.

"He'll be back. I bet he just ran out of smokes and went to find a place to get a pack. Knowing him, he's bound to run into all sorts of trouble in the meantime."

The rapid expansion of my companionship in this ridiculous bar seemed poised to cast a new light on the evening. I looked back and forth at the two women. Elsie was a lean, bouncy collegiate, a blend of hippy and hipster (more the first than the second) with a warm smile and gaze. She seemed the type that boys quickly fell in love with, partly or mostly because she could draw them in but keep them from achieving that ultimate closeness that borders on possession. The effect of this attraction/repulsion mechanism was plain to see on poor Paul, now lost in the snow.

I have a harder time describing Claire. She was, it could be said, much cooler in temperature—at least in her idling position, to use an automotive metaphor that would have made Horak cringe (Horak hated when the body was compared to a machine). In contrast to Elsie, Claire stood behind a series of walls, which far from discouraging the barbaric hordes challenged them to attempt a breach. And so the pattern was clear: attack, repulsion, siege, eventual penetration and occupation, abandonment. There were no small affairs for Claire. She seemed to have been thoroughly shaken on more than one occasion, brought down, as it were, to the very bottom, at which point she'd scratch and climb her way back up, bathe, dress, and mount a barstool somewhere to indicate a continuation of her reign. Apart from all this, I was starting to find some sort of karmic tranquility in the idea that it might be Claire who at least had a shot to take my father's place between those cinderblocks.

We made some small talk. Claire asked Elsie what she and Paul were doing on their night away from the college.

"We're having a couple of drinks here and then heading to a friend's party in town."

"Sounds great," said Claire, "at least a lot better than fretting about my interview."

"You're more than welcome to join. You guys can also come along if you want. The more the merrier."

"Thanks for the offer," Gabe said, "but Sy and I have some things to talk about. We haven't seen each other in a while."

"Why not?" Elsie asked with wonderfully blithe indifference to the heap of refuse swept under that particular carpet.

"Because I've been away," I cut in, "for twenty years."

"And you never visited him?"

"Never," said Gabe.

"Ginny mentioned that your wife started the theater with you. She said your wife was one of the best students she ever had."

Gabe looked over at me with a peculiar expression. "It's true," he said, more to himself or me than to Elsie, "when she was a student she loved everything, every book, every play, every damn line. She just absorbed everything and let it churn inside of her until some idea or notion or vague feeling emerged and pointed in a direction. Any direction. A beam of light into a dark corner somewhere, a corner that you didn't even know existed. You know how she was, Sy, you know what she was—who she was."

Claire and Elsie looked over at me. "I did," I said, "I used to know her, but that was a long time ago."

"These things don't change. They either stay the same forever or they change so fundamentally that the person doesn't exist anymore."

"Well," Elsie said, obviously the bolder of the two, or just the more optimistic, "I'd love to meet her." Gabe, it seemed to me, struggled to maintain his composure by repeatedly rubbing the palm of his free hand over his face.

Claire, probably sensing that the gathering was quickly coming apart at the seams, drained the remaining two-thirds of her drink in one tilt and rose from her chair. "I really should be getting to bed. Thanks for the drink and the company. And tell your father that I send him my very best wishes."

"Wait," I said, springing up after her, "can't you stay a little longer? We just sat down."

"I'd better not. I don't want to embarrass myself tomorrow."

"Doing what?" asked Gabe.

"Claire's interviewing for my old man's spot."

Gabe, who'd been (and perhaps still was) quite close with my father, said to my surprise, "Then we should have one drink in Walt's honor."

"I guess," Claire said. "It's hard to resist if you put it like that."

Gabe went to the bar and put in the order. When he got back to the table, Elsie said, "Did Ginny tell you that we're performing *Snowfall* next October? She just cast it together with the spring play."

"She told me."

"I'll be playing Milli."

Gabe nodded and took a sip of his beer. By all accounts *Snowfall* was his best work and Ida had been the original and perhaps the one and only truly authentic Milli, a Milli who walked off stages in New York, Minneapolis, San Francisco and elsewhere to universal praise. He wrote the play some ten years ago, well after that painful winter of 1997. It made Gabe's name, and for a brief period, culminating with the reception of many awards and stories about him and Ida in various local and national papers, it made him famous, which was probably too much for the modest Gabe Slatky. It was also, as far as I know, the final time Ida took the stage. After the buzz around *Snowfall* reached its height and started to fade, sometime, I'd say, around 2005 or maybe early 2006—so during that long haul between the second and third drafts of *Blue, Red, Gray*—I bought a copy of the play, which was no easy thing to find and have shipped to Prague in those days, believe it or not. I remember precisely when it came in the mail. If I close my eyes and think of it, I can see my hand reaching into the mailbox and pulling out that thin brown envelope. For some reason, my hands started to tremble, or outright shake for god's sake, when I ripped open the package and pulled out the book. It had been one of those terrible weeks of weather in Prague—gray, damp and as cold as hell. There's no sense going into detail about the goings-on with Horak at that point. Suffice it to say, problems abounded, with each problem leading to delay, delay, delay! It was dark when I took *Snowfall* together with a larger than normal glass of whiskey and sat down in my second-hand armchair. I opened it. The dedication to Ida resounded on the first page: *My muse, my beloved.*

I continued past this formidable obstacle, despite the fact that my first reaction was a desire to hurl the thin volume into a blazing fire somewhere and watch the thing burn into ash, pretending that I had destroyed not a copy of the thing but the thing itself, and in so doing had destroyed him, Gabe, and their love. *My muse, my beloved!* For the briefest of moments, she was my muse, my beloved. Brief. Impossibly brief.

Two characters rose off the page, a sister and a brother named Milli and Karl. The play, in structure, was simple— in other words, typically Slatkian. The sibling's mother has just died, leaving Milli and Karl parentless. Jointly, they've inherited a rustic lakeside cabin. Karl has recently quit his job as a high school teacher and moved into the cabin, leaving behind his wife, who's called Milli for help. There are some references to Karl's rejection of the war in Iraq, that his leaving of his life behind is some sort of protest against the collective social endeavor of war, though this is never directly stated. It seems clear, whether or not it is in the end an anti-war play, that Karl is experiencing something like a crisis of morality. But this isn't the full picture. The moral crisis seeps into other dimensions, some intimate, others bordering on the metaphysical. The play opens with Milli pushing open the door of the cabin and entering the space, a space we don't leave the remainder of the play's single, long scene. I don't see the point of getting into the nitty-gritty about the play. The dialogue coupled with the precise emotional fluctuation ranks with the best of O'Neill. I'd even say the play was pure O'Neill, maybe purer O'Neill than O'Neill himself.

"It's an amazing part," Elsie said. "I'd love to be able to talk about the role with Ida one of these days, maybe before summer, since I plan on mastering the lines over break. It's a demanding role—physically and emotionally."

"It's a marathon, for sure," I added, maybe (if I'm being honest) in order to elicit the following response from Gabe.

"I didn't realize you'd seen it."

"I read it."

"I wouldn't have thought you would."

"Why wouldn't he?" Claire asked as Chuck set down the round of drinks.

Gabe and I stared at each other. I was genuinely interested and also nervous about how he'd respond. It's likely he felt the same and the moment devolved into an old-fashioned, childish staring contest. Claire's question seemed to hover there over the table.

"The better question is how a person could not read it," Elsie cut in. "I mean, and I'm not intending to flatter, but the play is fucking awesome."

I kept my eyes fixed on Gabe. He was around thirty when *Snowfall* became such a big success. It seemed like the beginning for him. Now, ten years later, it rather looked like an endpoint, the end of a startling period of youthful vision and drive. It was a drive not only after a mastery of a craft, it was an attempt at—a reaching toward—the very essence of art itself: aesthetic perfection. And *Snowfall* comes close. If it misses at all, it's a matter of a fraction of a degree in one direction or another. It's a tension that might fade a bit too soon or too late, a history that encroaches a little too much or not enough, a sibling love that at times seems a little too unconditional, perhaps a little too erotic. Make no mistake, these are hardly perceptible flaws and in some ways these "flaws" ultimately give the piece its human quality and thus the flaws are not really flaws at all but reminders, signposts, that however much *Snowfall* is a work of art, it is also very much a moment of life, real, unaesthetical, ugly, horrible, absurd and beautiful life. After *Snowfall,* Gabe basically didn't write again. I mean, he wrote some new plays, words appeared on paper, but he didn't *write* in the transcendent meaning of the term. And Ida never acted again. Not once. I sat in that basement bar and tried to make sense of these things, tried to understand why this very simple fact had never occurred to me before. *Snowfall* was a dividing line.

"By the way," Elsie said to Gabe, "I love how you describe the snowfall in the play. That part when Milli just goes on and on about it for like two pages as Karl sits there by that cast iron stove—the images of hot and cold all mixed up together, his silence contrasting with her monologue, the juxtaposition of male and female, so many layers. I mean, I feel that scene in my body just thinking about it. There's something so, well, so lustful about that scene."

The effects of this last line rippled across the table. Claire fussed a bit with her collar, sliding the index and middle fingers of her left hand beneath it and onto the skin of her neck, a gesture that seemed to me a habitual nervous reaction. Gabe lifted his bowed head and gazed over at Elsie with a peculiar, glazed expression on his face. He looked not at her, it seemed, but through her for some fifteen or twenty seconds, long enough for me (and her, I think) to start feeling a rising anxiety about how he might react. Then he drank some beer, finishing the remains of one and beginning the fresh one Chuck had just brought over. Then he shook his head. "You're right. Lust. That was what I felt when writing it. The purest possible lust, surrender to the flames. A fire of body and soul."

My god, the way Elsie looked at that moment!

"That's incredible," she said.

Claire looked over at me, trying to puzzle out, I imagine, how I was reading this exchange.

"It's incredible," Elsie continued, "that Paul and I just randomly stumbled into this place and met you guys. I can't wait to tell Ginny about it."

"Listen," I said, "maybe from your perspective it's incredible, but from ours there's actually nothing incredible about it. We're here for a reason."

"What's the reason?" Claire asked.

"What?"

"The reason. The occasion why you're here?"

"I . . . I . . ."

"He doesn't know," Gabe cut in, "and neither do I."

"How strange," Claire said.

"Maybe there isn't a reason," Elsie added. "Can't two old friends meet without a reason? Meet just to meet?"

Gabe abruptly stood up from the table. All eyes focused on him. "Excuse me," he said.

Claire glanced down at her watch. Elsie's eyes shifted back and forth between Gabe and the door that led into the stairwell and out onto the street. Perhaps she was expecting Paul to return at any moment, though whether she feared or hoped for his return, I have no idea. For his part, Gabe seemed unsure of his next move. He clearly wanted to flee the table, but fleeing the table would have

63

meant fleeing the bar, which in turn would have necessitated, given his stated aversion to all other bars, a return home—home to Ida, who would probably still be up at this relatively early hour. She would be there awake in the guestroom, silent, forlorn, emotionless, lonely, and gone gone.

"Come on," I demanded, "sit back down. Sit down."

As I said this, sensing Claire's renewed desire to leave, I reached out and put a hand on her arm to signal that she should stay as well, that staying and leaving would have to be done in concert. Plus, to be honest, I sensed that sides were forming and that Claire was on my side.

Gabe sat, lifted his beer and took a long drink. As he set the glass back down on the table he said, "I'd like to hear about Horak now, about the book."

"I wouldn't want to bore the others," I said, fishing for their endorsement. I wanted nothing more than to talk about Horak and the book that I'd spent seventeen years of my life transforming into an English that could only be described as resplendent.

"I'd also love to hear," said Claire as she fixed her eyes on me in a way I took to be, or at least wanted to be, flirtatious.

How could I have resisted, despite what I perceived as a lack of support from Elsie, who clearly wanted to remain focused on her upcoming role as Milli. At the same time, Gabe had asked to hear, which meant that by definition the result of that request must be of interest to her. Or am I making Elsie into a caricature here? She was young, probably twenty-one years old. She was sexy, no doubt about it. She was enthusiastic and smart, maybe threateningly so. Lustful, she'd said. This single word seemed more insightful than anything I'd thought about Gabe's play and perhaps more than anything I'd ever thought about any work of literature, Horak's magnum opus included. Lustful. A wolfish, wild and untameable lust injected into a most domesticated, civilized heart.

I looked around the bar, trying to think of how to start. The hockey crowd remained locked in place in front of the large television set. Around tables and on stools, people sat with their drinks, some alone, some in pairs or groups. Paul's jacket hung from his abandoned spot.

It seems to me to matter that it's getting deeper into the night as I write this. Perhaps the focus on Elsie's use of "lustful" is indicative of the sort of degeneration of my narrative control. Psht! I don't aspire to any! On some level, I'd like nothing more than for another person to break into my apartment, tie me up, and finish writing this account in my name, especially because I'm on the verge of an embarrassingly long monologue, perhaps the longest in the

65

sad history of that musty, horrible bar. The length of the thing is not a conscious choice, just as the length of Horak's masterpiece was not for its own sake but because the subject demanded it. I could have said nothing or everything and for reasons both magnanimous and hideously narcissistic I chose the latter. I'll try my best to give an accurate picture of the scene, though given my mid-level intoxication and my concern for how Claire and Elsie (and of course Gabe!) were taking the account, I can't vouchsafe absolute fidelity. But why on god's green earth would anyone ever want that!

"It was late evening when Josef Kostel arrived in Prague. Dusk had turned the golden city gray, then grayer, then almost black. Nobody knew Josef there; he knew nobody. That's how Horak's novel begins. As you can tell, the opening is a reference to the beginning of Kafka's *Castle*—to K. arriving in the village, a stranger among the people there. This first line alone, I should point out, would have been enough (was enough), apart from all the rest, to result in the book's ban. A direct reference to Kafka, to K., to the world of the castle authority and its hinterlands, was seen as a direct provocation, an element of radicalism in need of immediate and forceful snuffing out. Since Stalinist times, the authorities had suppressed Kafka. And the censors, some of whom knew Kafka to the word, would have seen the

reference as clear as day had Horak tried to publish it with a state-approved publisher, which of course he never considered for a second.

"Imagine it. Imagine Josef Kostel arriving in Prague in the summer of 1919. He's from somewhere else— somewhere beyond the city, from out there, from away, from the depths of the countryside, from the periphery, the very edge of existence. Nobody knew him in Prague; he knew nobody. For that matter, Kostel itself was an invention. His real name was Salomon. The change from Salomon to Kostel was a sign of the times, the death of the empire ruled from Vienna, the birth of the Prague republic. Kostel has a past, at least compared with Kafka's K., who reveals only quick flashes of memory and nothing more—climbing a wall, planting a flag as a boy—of another village, a village resembling this new, strange village, but different, utterly different. Kostel has come to the capital. It's both a medieval and a totally new city. It's a city undergoing one of its many re-makings—now the capital of a new state, Czechoslovakia—a city no longer in the shadow of Imperial Vienna. He has with him artifacts of the past, pieces, scraps: a photograph (later to be hastily burned) of his parents and younger sister, a set of horse-hair paint brushes stolen from an artist's studio in Caorle around the time of the Battle of Piave River, a set of stone-carving knives from the same studio in Caorle, a fine Italian silk suit (also plundered), a *sidor* printed in Zagreb and acquired who knows when from who knows where, and two thin silver candleholders of Ottoman lineage.

"Josef Kostel had spent about a year as a front soldier in the imperial army and was part of the campaign on the Italian front, though it is unclear whether or not he fought in the disastrous battle on the Piave River. We know he was in Caorle around the time. We know he got those brushes there and that stone-carving set. But who was that anonymous artist—the man painting seascapes of the Adriatic, carving tiny busts of Franz Joseph, later of Mussolini? On his way north after the peace, Kostel found himself in the company of an older man named Karl Osterhase. Osterhase doesn't appear until later in the novel—and then only in a dream—but no matter. This book isn't a straightforward thing. It zigzags and spirals. Osterhase tells Josef that the end of the empire means a total breakdown of order. Everything was up for grabs. People who stood out needed to blend in, Germans in Bohemia and Silesia, Hungarians in Romania, and Jews everywhere in New Europe. One's future survival, Osterhase tells Josef, depends first and foremost on one's ability to disappear and then to reappear as someone else. Before reaching Vienna, Josef burns his pa-

pers. In a fire among a Gypsy camp outside the city, Josef
Salomon goes up in flames. The man from out there, from
nowhere, from everywhere east and west, north and south,
the wanderer, is lost in the smoke of history. In Vienna,
Osterhase takes Josef to see a man named Oswalt Friedl, a
doctor of forgery, who from the ashes of Salomon brings
Kostel to life, Josef Kostel, a Catholic, a man from Prague.
Everything had to be supplied: birth certificate, baptismal
records, army papers, and so on, but none of this was a
problem for Friedl, who possessed a large apothecary's cab-
inet of official stamps. This was a rebirth. Josef Kostel was
born, age 19, religion Catholic, place of birth Prague, parents Jan and Magda, education the Academy of Fine Arts
Vienna, profession artist."

I paused and looked at my companions—Gabe,
Claire, and Elsie. I didn't want to stop. I couldn't stop.
The story came pouring out of me.

"A new man, a new capital city, a new state—as if the
whole world had just exploded and then was in the process of settling down again as dust settles. It was a sort of
apocalypse, perhaps, though seemingly without any meaning. Apocalypse it had been on the Piave River where Josef
Salomon—still Salomon, still a Jew, still from out there
in the countryside—made his way through the carnage of
some 200,000 casualties to Caorle where he found that

shop and took his set of brushes and carving tools. The apocalypse on the western bank of the Piave River, where tens of thousands found themselves cut off from supplies and reinforcements. How did he make it back again while so many others, over 20,000 by some estimates, died trying to cross back to the eastern shore? Of course, Piave! It was the fatal blow to the empire, the glorious empire of Vienna, the empire that had saved Europe from the Turks and from Luther, the empire of Charles V, Metternich, Maria Teresa, and Franz Joseph. That empire died on the banks of the Piave River and one could say that Salomon died there, too. Names were dying all over Europe in those days. German names died and gave way to Italian names, Hungarian names, Slovenian names. The book of names— this is what gave a person life year after year, to be written in the book of names.

"Josef Kostel arrived in Prague late in the evening. He'd come from Vienna with his freshly stamped documents. He knew nobody in the city of his re-birth—not a soul. He set off from the train station to find a place to spend the night.

"Don't worry, I'm not going to tell you the day-by-day, moment-by-moment story of Josef Kostel, and Horak doesn't either. It's just that this moment of arrival is so incredibly rich, vivid, and full. Horak weaves a detailed tapestry around the moment for something like sixty pages. The opening chapter of the novel is nothing but the arrival of the stranger Kostel. As you'd expect, it was the first part of the novel that he wrote. He began it already in 1971 and finished the first draft of the 'The Arrival' in February 1972. Alena, his wife, then typed half a dozen copies, one of which was buried in the Horakovi garden in a village near Třeboň. One copy, of course, Horak kept locked in his desk under a false bottom of the lower left drawer. The others found their way through channels into the underground.

"Believe me, none of this is tangential. The novel as it ended up and the process of creating the novel and the ways in which the novel reached its readers are deeply intertwined. All of it is absolutely epic. The novel itself covers some thirty-five years, the writing of the novel close to twenty. The translation now seventeen! Pages filtered out, chapters moved from the world into the shadow world. Imagine if some of these pages fell into your hands. They could have been written at any time, yesterday, years before, a decade in the past. And you'd read them and search out more, and more, and more. You'd get them hopelessly out of order, the plot careening this way and that, forward and back. Dozens of chapters, hundreds and hundreds of pages. Imagine the experience of reading this thing—this

otherworldly thing year after year and in no particular order from 1971 until 1989, reading just whatever happened
to fall into your hands from one day to the next. And
then think, too, about the illegal nature of the affair—
those pages burning in your hands. You devour and cherish them (maybe even copy them) before you need to pass
them on to the next in line, the next reader, the next
brother or sister in that semi-invisible society of opponents
of the regime. This is the myth of the novel, the myth that
perhaps more than any other element drove its fame. Not
that the fame and attention are undeserved. Far from it.
The work is absolutely brilliant. Still, no amount of brilliance can compare to the creation of a myth with its thousands or even tens of thousands of anonymous believers.

"Josef Kostel—he finds a place to spend that first night,
a dingy pension full of shady characters, more than a
few of them wayward ex-soldiers like himself. With just
a few graceful brushstrokes Horak paints the scene—an
encounter with a prostitute in an exceedingly cramped
vestibule, a stained-glass portrait of Cyril and Methodius
framed by a series of mossy green rectangles, the steep staircase, the old and dirty mattress resting on a creaky iron
frame, a mirror worn out and warped, the rusty handles of
the faucet in the room's sink, the filthy, moldy sink bowl.
The manager asks him how many nights he'll stay. A few,

Kostel tells him, maybe more, maybe forever. Kostel is a young man, thin from the war years and from struggling his way through Vienna as the Spanish Flu raged in the city. Thin, angular face, dark hair, dark eyes, pale skin. Not tall but not short either. A bit lank but still sturdy. Big hands. Long fingers.

"This is a man without a past—and who can be such a man? His former self had been highly educated, though in a single relentless direction. He had been raised as a Talmudic scholar but quit his studies at age fifteen when he fell headlong first into mysticism and from mysticism into art. After that, his father had given up on him and told him to make his own way in the world. That was the beginning of the end of Salomon. During the next years, wherever and whenever he could, he'd gain some skills as a painter, and it was the promise of the war to take him to Italy—to the very center of the artistic realm—that convinced him not to flee from the draft. In the end, what he took from Italy was not knowledge but equipment. It was in Vienna, the city of Schiele, Klimt and Kokoschka, where he found the first tremors of his style.

"The next morning he pawned his candle holders for enough to pay for a week in the pension, to eat and drink reasonably well, and to buy a set of paints and a roll of canvas. During the following days, always between noon and evening, Josef hired the prostitute he encountered during his first evening at the house to sit for him. It didn't take much—a meal, a few pennies, a sample now and then of his work, charcoal treatments, light contour drawings, and finally a single finished oil, the latter a raw and rough piece that confronted the viewer with an audacious sexuality wrapped in intertwining, diaphanous silks. This was no coy image. It was brutal. And that's why Horak spends time on it, takes us onto and then under that lace, across that terrain of skin, between those thighs, over those cherry lips. It might be called pornographic, if it also wasn't somehow blurred, somehow off-kilter—and all the more sublime because of it. It was no work of genius; Kostel was not yet capable of that. Maybe Salomon had been capable of genius as he worked his way through mishnah and the swampy grounds of midrash to reach toward the Light. The painting, rather, was boldness and daring, an unfettered pursuit of sensibility. He made about a dozen paintings of the prostitute Lala and gave the best one—perhaps the only decent one—to her as payment for their final sitting.

"The pension was a place for wanderers and semi-criminals. Josef was eager to move on. Presenting himself in his Italian suit, giving the impression of a man of at least modest means, Josef managed to rent a small apartment just to the east of the National Theater, not far from the river Vltava. He'd left his address at the pension for Lala and she began to visit him a few times each week, not in order to practice her trade but because he'd become something like a friend. They'd pass nights and at times early mornings drinking schnapps at Josef's rickety table, discussing art, poetry, the city, war, sex—just about everything but their respective pasts. They had no past. No lineage. No history.

"It goes without saying that Josef lusted after her. After all, she was gorgeous, even if somewhat sickly and way too thin. She had a hard life, serving three or four customers a day just to barely scrape by. The competition was fierce, especially in the years after the war when the economy was in shambles and thousands of people thought that they'd be better off making a go of it in the city. Many of the newcomers turned to prostitution, driving down the prices for even the most desired girls. The whole city in those years seethed with transactional sex. Josef lusted. He might even have loved. But what's the difference, Horak asks, between the two? All lust turns to love, all love propped up by a pedestal of fiery desire. He tried to seduce her. She rebuffed him, telling him that by now she was disgusted by sex, fed up with the panting and grunting and clumsy thrusting. She only allowed herself to be painted over and over as Josef lurched unevenly toward a style, a form. And by the way, she told him, she'd sold that first painting he'd given her for a fine price—a price worth nine or ten clients or about three days of life—to an art dealer, who ran a gallery on the Náměstí Republiky.

"These newest paintings, infused by this lust/love, were better than the previous ones, which still had contained something of a prudish scowl, a self-critique and shyness. The brutality in the previous paintings had been one of condescension, perhaps even of a longing for the virgin beneath the work, for the essence of the mother to be redeemed from the wanton creature so starkly displayed. This next group of paintings contained the brutality, but it was a brutality of hardship within an aura of love, desire, friendship, respect, and admiration. The colors took on different hues and tints, merged and then separated in bold new ways, saturated with a purpose to reincarnate. Form melted and then reconsolidated with dynamic suggestion or a radical, spiritual longing. Lala came to life, his Lala.

"At some point when his money had been gone for weeks, when the possibility of survival seemed less than ever—less even in many ways than on the banks of the Piave—Josef hauled his six best Lalas to the dealer Leo

Steynberg, who'd bought that first painting after a night with Josef's muse. Steynberg was a major dealer with galleries in Vienna, Paris, Amsterdam and Prague. His biggest successes had been transnational exchanges—bringing eastern artists to the West, selling the Parisian stars to the men with money back in the east. He wasn't sure if Kostel would sell in Prague or Vienna, but he agreed to take the work to Paris. He could imagine a few Parisians he knew who'd be particularly interested in possessing his Lalas.

"But when the time came for Steynberg to take the paintings to Paris, Josef didn't want anyone else to possess Lala. She was now more or less living with him, though the relationship was never consummated. An intimate non-sexual or—as Horak would say—a sensual relationship formed, a relationship infused with a primordial sensuality that moved outward from the body and into the mind and then into the shared space and then dissipated and disappeared, all the while still remaining there in the body where it was first produced, first burned for fuel. Far from possession. There was no possession. It seemed to Josef that, if anything, Lala possessed his canvas, controlled his brush, and led his imagination into the uncontrollable blaze.

"In the end, Josef relented and let Steynberg take his Lalas to Paris for the opening of a show dedicated to the art of the east. He had little choice, badly needing the money from any sale. When he made the trip himself to Paris (ticket purchased by Steynberg) Josef found his Lalas surrounded by the works of Marc Chagall, Kazimir Malevich, Naum Gabo, Alexander Rodchenko, Nathan Altman, and many more. It was a huge show—almost a fair—radical, dynamic, everything Josef had dreamed about when he thought of Paris. Lost in this vast ocean of creativity were his Lalas, seemingly of a style out of step with the newest trends. They seemed more reflective of a previous era, the era before the war when the world still seemed ruled by a self-congratulatory, desperate, decadent, morose and wayward bourgeoisie.

"All the Lalas sold. Steynberg had the entire Parisian art-buying class lined up with their wallets open, wanting everything available in the show. It was the east, the wild east, which so titillated Parisian society. And though Josef's Lalas were stylistically outmoded, in many ways derivative, they still had something fresh about them and were stamped by uniqueness that comes from real, authentic passion. For Lala. For love.

"Don't get it wrong," I said and took a quick drink from my beer, "Josef didn't pine away for her in Paris. He was out just about every night to the early hours of the morning. He tried hashish and cocaine, frequented the cabarets, drank, danced, sang, celebrated life, free life, life as a man without history—a life floating on air. Days and weeks passed by. He sent Lala money for rent and then again a month later. In the meantime, he fell in love with an American named Mary Bankes, the twenty-four-year-old wife of Roger Bankes, a New York dealer connected with Steynberg. Roger was not yet thirty. He was the son of an industrialist and already, given his father's generous contribution to his starting capital, one of the biggest buyers in New York. No big buyer could do without Paris, and to Mary's delight Roger spent about half the year there. It was Mary who convinced her husband to buy all of Josef's pieces. She was enamored with them for the same reasons he was enamored with Lala, for the same reason he was now in love with her.

"They met at cafés. They drank whiskey and wine, smoked hashish mixed with tobacco, walked the streets, crossed the bridges, traversed the gardens and converged in his shabby hotel room. There, on the other side of those cheap mauve curtains, he seduced her, or she him, or both each other or themselves. Or, as Horak writes, it was the general seduction of time and space, blurring them, denying their existence, casting them out of the realm of desire. His Lala poured into her. She became his subject and object. In the early summer light, he painted her as she sat in an old, threadbare wing chair by the open window, the new hero of the modern world, the wife turned prostitute, the wife unbound, or as Horak writes, *the wife as warm wind rising.*

"Can you try to imagine what this must have done to the poor communist censors? An artist like Josef Kostel, a lover like Mary Bankes, Lala back in Prague. Paris in the foreground, New York in the background. It was a burst of flame, pure fire, into the ashen world of Czech normalization. Mary lingered in Paris for as long as she could after Roger returned to America. She'd learned to speak French as a child and was patient with Josef as he struggled to get along. She spoke no German or Czech, Josef no English. But this was Paris, a world away from all other tongues, a place as far away from the Czech language as seemed to Josef linguistically possible. For days on end, Mary Bankes could barely leave that room. She demanded to be painted, and repainted, and painted again until her whole body gave out and she couldn't endure, either physically or emotionally, to be painted even one more time. And she would collapse on the bed and dream her wild dreams.

"In the late fall, maybe in the middle of November (Horak could be quite unspecific about things like this) Mary Bankes boarded a ship bound for New York. Was she in love with Josef Kostel? Nobody knows. She probably didn't know herself. Horak would not reveal something that cannot possibly be revealed. She left in a cloud of ambiguity, promising one thing, then another, without the slightest bit of forethought about whether she'd really make good. And Josef? He soaked in these promises as he had once soaked in prayer. But he also knew that these were not promises for the keeping. Promises corrupted from the start by their vehemence. It was play-acting. Yes, this hotel room was the scene of a most brilliant play. Two characters. One long, uninterrupted scene lasting months, coming to an expected but still abrupt and jarring end. This is Horak. Horak gives us all this, layering one piece atop the next. Burying us.

" 'The world wants the exotic East,' Steynberg tells Josef after Mary leaves, 'it's tired of the Parisian grace, the cultivation of London, the materialism of New York, the confidence and boredom of civilization.' Wild and civilized. Wildness—a raw kinetic energy to replenish the atrophied heart of civilized man, a man clad in English wool, top hat and leather shoes. This is a world that needs Lala. Hundreds or hundreds of thousands of Lalas, an army of Lalas fighting in the shadows of the boulevards from Vienna to Paris, surfacing in New York, Chicago, and Soviet Moscow. Within days, those Lalas, which Roger Bankes had taken with him from Paris to New York, were gone from his Gallery of New European Art. A banker bought one. Two others went to a coffee importer, Brazilian by birth, and so on. The main thing was the speed, the voracious appetite. Bankes immediately telegraphed Steynberg: 'Get me all of Kostel's women.' He had quite the shock when those Mary Bankeses were unwrapped and unrolled but weeks after his flesh and blood wife arrived by steamship at Manhattan Island. How could he sell those paintings of his wife? But he did and for scandalous profits. His wife, the dignified, proper East Side lady, went—just like Lala—to the highest bidder.

"This is Horak at his best, tracing those crates of Marys as if following Mary herself. He leaves Mary, the real Mary. Her trip is of little consequence for us compared to the journey of those other Marys. And there is Josef, still in Paris, suddenly a prime horse in Steynberg's stable, a key link on the chain of commerce that runs East to West. Rawness. Cultivation. Consumption. And they ate those Marys for a midnight snack, secret, slumberous, there in the folds of darkness. This is Horak. This is Jan Horak! God, I can't possibly capture for you the intensity I felt when I first worked on that scene of Roger Bankes opening the crate from Steynberg and casting his eyes on his wife, a woman he was seeing—viewing, gazing at, perceiving, violating—for the very first time. Maybe he even had a fleeting glimmer of knowing her, knowing what he couldn't possibly have wanted to know: the depths of her desire. But he, Roger Bankes, is gone before we get to understand whether or not he's able to confront what he finds in that Pandora's box. He floats to the periphery, loses focus and then disappears, giving way to our man Josef Kostel. The Horakian lens has Josef rarely completely out of focus and almost never totally in focus. There's always some fuzziness, however slight, softness around the edges, as if the camera moved ever so subtly as the finger snapped the picture, a tiny flinch, nothing but a millimeter. A velvet fuzz.

"Josef feels like he could stay in Paris forever, that he might never return to Prague, to his filthy room, to his filthy Lala. And so he lingers month after month as his paintings keep flowing across the ocean, as money keeps flowing back. A year passes, then half of another. His French starts to push out his Czech. He's becoming a man of Europe, a man of the world.

"At the end of the second year, though, he did go back. Despite everything, and over the objections of Steynberg, he returned to Prague. Whether it was that life in Paris severed Josef from the wellspring of creativity he needed to survive, whether it was the crushing torment that came with his loss of Mary Bankes, or whether it was his longing for the ur-Mary, the primitive woman still inhabiting his internal and external chambers, whatever it was, there was a pull back east. It was a force like an undertow at the edge of the ocean, a force much like history itself. Or, Horak speculates, a force that propels us forward into the future and drives a person beyond history's grasp. It was all this. A pull. A propulsion.

"After two years away, Josef turns the key and his old door swings open with a creak of its joint. Who is this man? The question resounds, though it's not a question Horak asks directly. Like so much he does, it wells up from some underground source and then hovers over the scene like a mist or fog. The drugs, parties, sex of Paris now melt into dream—and what if the whole thing were just a dream anyway? A fantasy of all those scribblers and mark-makers: to be in Paris. Could Josef Kostel have been returning from a night out at the pub, which ended (as so many of Horak's nights would have without me) with him sleeping off his drunkenness under a tree in Kampa Park, a sleep full of visions of Paris and a woman who might have been named Mary Bankes and an art dealer, a Jew like he had formally been, who he'd named Steyn-berg with a y? Who could say for sure, as that door creaked open, if Lala ever existed? And if she did exist, was her name not Lala but Lydia, a Russian exile of the revolution and writer of children's books about tigers and bears in the fields and forests beyond that old stone house in the countryside—some countryside out there far beyond the swelling of the city? If Lydia existed he would have met her in Vienna as he trudged north after swimming his way nearly naked across the Piave River while around him 20,000 men drowned. Lydia, whose graying hair and aquiline nose, small body, and narrow hips and narrow shoulders made her look at once girlish and old. The door creaked and opened and Lala lay sleeping there on the bed, practically dead to the world. Heat pulsed from the small stove in the corner. An old second-hand blanket that he'd bought in a pawnshop was slipped about halfway down to the floor. The other half still clung the right side of her body, leaving the left side fully exposed. Her naked skin—at least compared to the American Mary Bankes or the Russian Lydia—seemed almost black, at the very least a deep earthy brown, sun-deepened, ripe. Her hair—tangled, loose, wild—concealed part of one cheek, the other one was buried in the pillow. Her face, in any case, was turned away from the door to the window. He approached and when he got close enough he could see the dryness on her lips. A wide nipple stuck up in the warm, humid air. Her chest moved up and down with each steady

85

breath. Josef considered waking her or lying down next to her in order to summon her dream into his, merging this and other realities, his Paris with her . . . what? He couldn't imagine where Lala would go in her oneiric wanderings, but they must have been places far away from here. And yet she didn't leave, as he didn't, but shared his bed night after night until she owned it, possessed it as she possessed him. Are you feeling Horak now?" I asked the others around me, though I continued without allowing them time to respond. "This stuff can't at all be compared to the fairly straightforward account in *Rain, Rain*. This is what I told my former friend Florian after I'd managed to claw my way through the book for the first time. I had to tell him that the book would challenge him precisely at his weakest point, that point where a sense of absolute self dissolves into thin air. And then I told him what I'm sure he already knew, that his translation of *Rain, Rain* into German (*Regen, Regen*) was a muddled, amateurish mess, which did significant damage to Horak's international reputation. Incalculable damage. Or maybe I called it what it truly was, a goddamn disaster and a tragedy and a literary homicide. Horak, who knows no German (or at least pretends to know none) felt the damage in the total arrhythmia of Florian's language—not to say that Horak is rhythmic—far from it. Far from it. But there's a difference between the two types of arrhythmia. And this is what I told Florian one night in Berlin, a disaster of a night for altogether different reasons. There is a difference, I said, between Schönberg and noise. Horak was Schönberg, Florian's *Regen, Regen* was the equivalent of the blare of that hockey game over there. Florian told me to go fuck myself, no surprise there. I was already half way out the door of the bar where I'd found him. I had little choice but to convince Horak to cancel his contract for *Blue, Red, Gray*, the result of which was that Florian threatened my life by late night SMS on at least three occasions. Still to this day, no German or any other translation but mine has been approved. So you see, there's nothing self-evident in it. The shift from Horak's sublime Czech into an average English is totally insufficient. The English needs to soar!

"Whichever Lala who's there, in whatever state she exists, she doesn't wake up when Josef comes in and drops his suitcase to the floor. This is no mere sleep, Josef thinks, but an opium sleep. The opium trance spills out of the room. The pungent odor calls to mind similar spaces he'd encountered in Paris, her body similar bodies. And here again, Horak displays his magic touch. The reader is already in such a heightened state, both because we've been anticipating the next encounter with Lala and because Horak has suspended us in a kind of middle zone between the real and the surreal, dream and wakefulness. Josef moves to the bed and sits down next to her body. He feels her hair: silken, ashen. He places a tip of his pinky finger on these dried-out lips, singed, no doubt, by the opium pipe. Ashes, ash and ash, the table in the corner is covered with a thin yellowish-black film of dust, as fine as powder. The pipe lies on its side next to the bed, tossed haphazardly away to make room for the demons of sleep. He's suddenly beyond tired. He lies down next to her, though there's barely room, and feels himself as small as a boy. He looks at his hands and notices that his fingers are stained yellow from rolling those pills of opium around in his fingers day after endless day. Dusk after endless dusk. The days unfolded into the underworld, into the realm of death, where visions of wild beasts like Lydia's tigers and bears mixed with the fantasy of being gripped between a sturdy set of American thighs. We can barely wait for Josef to wake up, lift his head from that small corner of pillow and tell us definitively, 'This is real, this is life.'

"We get no such relief but instead slip into a sort of perpetual surreal, if that's what we can call this state of ever-present uncanny that lasts for the remaining twelve hundred and fifty pages of the novel. Just consider this. Some two hundred pages into the book and we're forced to walk the rest of the way on a flimsy foundation of reality.

It's masterfully done and the reader, despite the discomfort, comes to love this new terrain. It's like walking on a beach that's constantly being reconfigured by the tides. It's probably when he reached this moment in the book, this profound transition, that the great Vaclav Havel wrote the words, 'Quite extraordinary,' on a lined note card and slipped it under Horak's door. The note card, of course, was unsigned—nobody signed anything those days—but if you saw it, you'd recognize Havel's handwriting immediately. It was September of 1976, I think, when the card appeared at Rieger Park. Just months before, Horak had sent the first batch of manuscripts containing the return from Paris into the underground. Havel and company saw what Horak was up to. They knew that the whole essence and atmosphere of society could change abruptly and fundamentally. The latest shift had occurred just a few years before as the relatively open 1960s gave way to the brutal, insipid return of ideological orthodoxy in the wake of the Soviet tanks. Normalization, it was called—pure Horakianism.

"Josef wakes up to a new day. Lala has vanished during this long sleep that seemed destined to never end. The sun came through the room's single window, causing the dust that rose into the air as he threw back the blanket to explode into a thousand tiny fireworks. Josef leaves the building, has a breakfast of coffee and rolls and then sets out (at least in a vague sense) to find Lala. This is the great 'Vítkov to Petřín Chapter,' as it came to be known in the dissident circles of the late 1970s and 1980s. If someone mentioned the 'Vítkov to Petřín Chapter,' it was a convenient code for Josef Kostel's long walk. It was much more than a walk; it was a process of self-discovery. He discovered his place not only in this new capital of a new nation in a Europe transformed, but also in some higher cosmological sense. It could be said that on this walk he really becomes Josef Kostel, though of course it's a problematic notion to become someone so recently invented. For the novel, the walk is also critical, because it sets the stage for the next four hundred pages and perhaps much more than that, certainly for those four hundred from the 1920s until the Nazi invasion in 1938. This whole section, on some higher level, could be termed 'the search for Lala,' a search never concluded and never abandoned.

"Josef Kostel, Horak writes, left his room and found himself on the Vítkov Hill. The chapter contains the walk of Josef Kostel through a topography that becomes mythic for the Czech underground. It begins on Vítkov, the great symbol of the Hussite challenge and Czech national resistance to foreign occupation and control. It's no mistake that the walk has a medieval beginning, or to be more precise a late medieval beginning with Kostel peering out at modern Prague—the past gazing into the present. Four hundred years in the past. What does this mean, this gazing through time, this peregrination through the mythological Czech past? Horak was no nationalist, at least not in any simple sense. He had a deep suspicion of nationalism as he had of everything else. And so when Kostel senses the spirit of Jan Žižka as he peers down on the city, there are many conflicting impulses at work. There's a neophyte's nationalism, for sure, one sparkling like the epaulettes of a new recruit. There's fatalism. We know that Žižka's movement failed, as the republic failed. On the other hand, Žižka fought while the Czechs in 1938 surrendered without resistance. The surge of Žižkovian spirit marks the beginning of the walk, not the end. And it could be said that the rest of the walk is the disintegration of the type of epiphany on Vítkov and a rise of a new type of being on the opposite side of the city. Ultimately, the walk is a rejection of Žižka, a rejection of the transcendent value of national or political identification—just as it as a questioning of the alternative, the radical supremacy of the self. The underground tried to appropriate both moments to use them for its own agenda. Horak could only stand back and gaze at the literary terrain.

"All manner of sights, sounds, textures are touched upon as Josef makes his way though the city. The walk has a history to it—a history of Central Europe—with his story, Josef's story, at the very heart. Literally and figuratively, Kostel descends into Prague. If you're ever in Prague, you'll know the labyrinth Josef enters, or at least the mental labyrinth, or both. The roaming poet, the history of Prague is full of them and Horak is playing with the idea of that figure here. But he's no poet, Josef. And he's barely Czech, speaking the language really quite poorly and with nowhere near the refinement of the contemporaneous street roamer Nezval. As readers, we have no precise date or even year for the walk from Vítkov to Petřín, which is itself a mini-*bildungsroman* or a surrealist play on the *bildungsroman* form. We weave through eras—the Hussite challenge, the German baroque, medieval Jewry in all its mystical and clashing garments, the rise of the bourgeoisie, the rise of the workers, who flood in from Žižkov and Holešovice.

"Josef perceives this seemingly endless layering. It's not only the layering of one social class upon the other, but religion on religion, epoch on epoch, style on style, identity on identity to the point that all notions of linear time crumble before his gaze. Hidden foundations of ancient ruins rise up to overtake the newest structures of steel, concrete and glass. Streets close in overhead and choke themselves off before opening yet again into wide, airy boulevards. You can imagine that a cubist sensation came over Josef as time and space unfolded, overlapped, and merged, as the unending movement of automobiles, trains, and streetcars mirrored or commented on the flow of the Vltava. The whir and scream of the breaking street-cars, the hum of the machines, and then the stasis: the gloomy Hradčany, the ruins of Vyšehrad, the statue of Hus, the cathedral of St. Vitus, the Church of Bethlehem, and the Jewish quarter. And out of the corner of his eye, he glimpsed the Old-New Synagogue, the sparkling Spanish Synagogue, and the Pinkas.

"No matter. The majestic quality of this section denies easy description or explanation. The point is that it takes the reader to the base of Petřín hill and then up to the top, where she or he can survey the whole city—the whole of Prague—with Josef Kostel, and can experience with him a moment of vision or awareness as he gazes out at life below. It's unclear from where it came, but the initial spark was a single notion: the seductive brutality of the modern condition.

"Even Josef doesn't know what this really means or where it came from. Seductive brutality. It was no fully formed philosophical idea. It was a direction—a thrust or desire generated by one of those enormous, self-indulgent, beautiful and dangerous questions. In this case, the question: what is the essence of modern life? And once that question is thrown down on the table, others follow, others flood in and try to crowd it out. But let's get back to the scene. Josef on the top of Petřín hill, the river moving below him, clouds gathering above, church bells resounding from every corner of the city, flocks of swifts and swallows massing and disintegrating, wheeling wildly in the eye of the setting sun, its orange rays drenching the city in pink light, setting the gilded crown of the National Theater on fire. Immerse yourself in this panorama. Feel Josef there. Feel him open up his arms. Feel him breathe that autumnal air. Feel him embrace the whole of the earth between the palms of his outstretched arms. And listen as he lets out his great primal scream, as if to say, as Horak writes, 'Now I live for the first time.'

"I'm sorry if I'm getting carried away," I said to my tablemates. "The walk from Vítkov to Petřín hill was one of my toughest sections. I spent years on it and—quite literally at times—wrestled with Horak over many difficult spots, especially when we confronted those trapdoors, underground passageways, escape routes, and even an old and forgotten landmine now and then. And the cry from

Petřín—what is this but one of the most astounding examples of undaunted individuality in the whole history of Communist Europe! As one dissident grimly remarked after reading this chapter, 'Now the guillotine will fall on the Raven of Rieger Park.' Yes, Horak was the raven. Why raven? It's unclear when it started and Horak claims no knowledge of how or why he got the moniker. Some say the name reflected his gangly gait and narrow face. Others claim that it had to do with his habit of stalking through the city after a night of drinking in the pubs, others his carnivorous diet. In my opinion, it comes from the story of Noah: 'Noah opened the window of the ark that he had made and sent out the raven; it went to and fro until the waters had dried up from the earth.' First, the raven, then the dove. Yes, this is it, this is critical, first Noah sent out the raven and then, and only then, he sent the dove.

"The profligacy and degeneracy of the previous painting is pushed to its utter limits in the aftermath of the walk from Vítkov to Petřín hill. New work emerges—raw, elemental and imbued with a crude and authentic egotism that sees in its own being the totality of being. Portraits of others give way to self-portrait, self-analysis, self-critique, and self-discovery. The raven flies! The raven soars! It surveys the whole known world from horizon to horizon, traces the gentle curve of all existence and reflects it in the curve of its eye.

"Steynberg wanted none of it. It was not Josef Kostel whom his buyers wanted to see depicted on canvas in bent, distorted forms. They clamored for more Lalas, more Mary Bankeses. But Lala had disappeared into one of those urban folds, like the wearing away of a city map. And Mary Bankes—long gone, a specter of a different world. The walk from Vítkov to Petřín hill might have been the culmination of his search for Lala. But if that's true, it's true only in a secondary sense, an adjunct sense. The search for Lala was the search for himself, for Josef Kostel, itself a fabrication of Osterhase and Friedl, a stamped page, a forged document, and on and on. I know, I'm moving back and forth. But it, too, moves like this, both the novel and the Raven. This is why it's simply one of the most difficult books to translate in the history of modern literature. And maybe to and fro with the raven, Noah's raven, is a good way of thinking about it. The landmarks guide us—the arrival in Prague, the Paris hotel room with Mary Bankes, the return to a sleeping Lala, the walk, the cry from Petřín, and Friedl's official stamps hitting the pages: bang, bang, bang!

"The years of the republic move like the raven. Speed combines with slowness, society with loneliness, love with

96

utter and absolute isolation. But consider—hold in your mind—the ferocity with which Kostel worked and lived. At the same time, you can feel the burden he carried. Periods of intense labor culminated in nervous breakdown and flight to the Grünhofberg Sanatorium in Austria. At some point during this vortex, Josef meets a new dealer named Melchior Kollar, every bit as proletarian as Steynberg was aristocrat. Kollar, who operated out of a run-down space in Malá Strana, had an eye for radicalism, an eye that seemed to be instinctually repulsed by standard notions of beauty or form. This could have been, Josef once considered, a consequence of being born with a deformed left hand. Kollar's conditions were draconian. He demanded sixty percent of every sale, not that there were many for Kostel, who didn't sell enough even to remain alive. He supplemented this meager income by taking commissions—a bust here, a portrait there—for the new rich and by giving private drawing and painting lessons to mostly young, unmarried bourgeois girls.

"The communist censors, who were always some of the first to get their hands on the latest Horakian releases, would have seen the meaning here. This is the struggle of the individual as creative actor, the creator of his own spiritual and material reality. This is the apotheosis of the human being, man as his own god. Even the exploitative Kollar is semi-heroic in this regard, daring to display the most shocking works, which the respectable galleries (including Steynberg's) refused to hang. And another thing these censors hated was Horak's portrayal of technology. There's no doubt that he's casting back a later environmentalism into the technology-obsessed 1920s and 1930s. We see in one scene a blinding electric light flooding into a copse of trees in a hidden courtyard below Hradčany. In another moment, a gray film descends from a seemingly heavenly or demonic source to black out a vibrant display of color. Ashen. Ash and ash. The world was ash—foretelling of the years to come, the war years, when everything would turn to ash around him.

"And what about love during these years of hardship and bold creation and bold imagination? Love. Josef falls in love about halfway through this section. It's a love that blends together with art and that ultimately, I would say, transcends it and exists as its own thing, able to breathe beyond the bubble of creative genius. Is Josef Kostel a genius? What a question! Horak would be absolutely livid if he heard this kind of talk. Horak has no patience for the term, calling it Romantic German garbage. Horak was a vicious hater of all things German. Despite his love of beer, he would never think of imbibing a German one, would never allow a piece of German sausage to touch his lips. For that matter, Horak wouldn't drink an American beer either. Once, coming back from a trip to New York, I brought him a six-pack of some trendy Brooklyn micro-brew. No sooner had he taken a sip of the first bottle then he violently spat it out onto the floor and wiped his mouth with his sleeve in disgust. I ended up drinking the rest of the pack myself that night while Horak consumed at least a dozen half-liter bottles of Pilsner.

"Josef Kostel in love. Maria. She was the daughter of a Slovak banker, who'd recently moved from Bratislava to Prague. His wife had died before the war, leaving him alone with four children, Maria being the youngest. She was no older than twenty when she first met Josef. She was studying oriental languages at the university at the time as one of the first female students ever admitted to the program, which, despite her formidable talent no doubt had something to do with the richness of her father. In her third year, more for relaxation than anything else, she started to come to one of Josef's drawing lessons. An orientalist. By age twenty, Maria was proficient in Greek, Latin, Hebrew, Arabic and Aramaic—not to mention modern languages like German, French, English, Czech and her native Slovak. She loved languages, loved the elegance of the characters, the script, the calligraphy, which made her want to learn even more, like Japanese and Chinese. Her father was a devout Catholic and tolerated Maria's linguistic passions as long as they stayed on the page. And even though Josef was Catholic—at least on paper—his impecunious life as an artist totally disqualified him from being a potential suitor for Maria. But traditional family life was far from their thoughts. Maria, this girl of twenty, was set—to put it euphemistically and perhaps ridiculously—on the attainment of unbridled eros, a project Josef wholeheartedly endorsed.

"If you'd come across just the first half of the book in the 1980s, as Horak was in and out of prison, being constantly interrogated and investigated, put on trial for one offense or another, you might have thought that the main thrust of the book was a call for a return to the glory of the first, free and democratic Czechoslovak Republic. And you can definitely see and feel this. The reader senses Horak's glamorization of the time. And yet, the reading is entirely wrong. The state is shown—no, the entire epoch is shown—as unstable, fragile, divided and ultimately too weak to withstand great challenges, including the greatest challenge of the century, Hitler's Germany. The love affair with Maria can only be understood in this context, as an allegory for those frenzied years before the decades of crisis, invasion, occupation, foreign domination, humiliation and tragedy.

"Divisions. Turmoil, a chaotic frenzy of the churning and remaking of life on an individual and collective basis. Josef Kostel, Jew from the countryside, transformed into a Catholic Czech from Prague. Maria Rybková, Slovak linguist who tried but failed to shed her Slovak tongue when out in refined Prague society together with her rich but provincial father. Juraj Rybka—fat, bald, tempestuous, sweaty, as anti-German as he was anti-Semitic, a true hater—of Jews, Germans, communists, socialists, anarchists, Hungarians, Ruthenians, and Gypsies. He had a begrudging respect for Austrians, especially the lords and barons of Vienna, and a genuine admiration for the British and Americans, though he hated them all, too. And you might think that Horak would simply have his way with this unseemly character. Not true! This was always Florian's mistake. Florian led the reader into realms that weren't there. The main thing about Rybka is that he's real—horrifyingly real, material, so present on the page that he seems to lift off of it with his pudgy face and hairy back. He's sweat and dirt and stubby fingers and gold. This is no realism in the sense of Dickens. Rybka and all the rest—it's totally Horakian. Completely its own thing. Horak is only Horak—nothing else.

"Eros rises around the reader, envelopes the reader in its fog, an eros woven around Horakian realism. Ut-

terly sensual. No sentimentality. Horak is incapable of it—
especially during these earlier years—despite giving Maria
what some might consider sentimental characteristics, like
her endearing Slovak accent, her domineering father, her
stifled creativity, her oppressed but gargantuan intellect,
and finally (and especially) her penchant for illness. I'll
take you into the key scene, a scene that forms the perfect
aesthetic counterpoint to the primal scream from Petřín
hill. The narrator, of course, stays close to Josef in mind
and body. By now it's years into the relationship. It's been a
hard few months for Josef. No sales, few customers, money
running low, nerves frayed, conflicts with Kollar leading
to Josef pulling all of his works from the gallery. Maria
has become engaged to the scion of another wealthy family from Bratislava. Despite this, her affair with Josef continues with the same intensity as before. And then she's
struck with an acute and extreme fever, followed by a crip-
pling weakness in the legs. Her father sends her out of the
city to a clinic near Brno. She writes to Josef, imploring
him not to write or call. Weeks pass. She writes again. 'I'm
dying. The doctors won't tell me the truth, but I'm sure of
it. I feel it in my body. I'm dying, Josef.' Now here's the
scene, a Horakian masterpiece, one reminiscent of Kafka's
'In the Cathedral' from *The Trial*. Josef is in great, great distress, utter distress—a crumbling, crushing state of mind.

At some point after receiving the letter, he goes to a cathedral for the first time since his conversion. By now, we've more or less forgotten that this is Salomon, student of the Talmud. Close to five hundred pages separate then from now.

"Kostel takes a seat in one of the pews. A dim light comes in through the side windows, illuminating, though just barely, the gilded capitals, richly painted walls, and the gloomy domed ceiling. Josef peers up into the space, which vanishes into a pit of darkness. After a while, he closes his strained eyes, bows his head and tries to pray for Maria, for her health, for her life. Or at least he tries to simulate prayer as he imagines it's done in a place like this. There are a few others in the rows in front and beside him, but they don't seem to be paying him any attention. He doesn't give them much thought either other than to register how ordinary it seems they sit in what for him was utter strangeness. Nothing else, he thinks, is like the interior of such a place. As he bows his head, he tries to think of precisely that—this space, this place. He thinks of Jesus on the cross, but can't hold the thought steady. It vanishes from him into irreality. Iconic frames emerge, the last supper, the final judgment, the resurrection of Lazarus. Yes, Lazarus. He pauses. He thinks of the Piave River and how none of those 20,000 was delivered from a watery death. None brought back to life. Except perhaps for him? But was he really there on the Piave River? Memory seems to collapse for him, itself as deep and dark as that fold of buttress above him, as endless, as nonexistent.

"Jesus. Jesus Christ. Son of God. Son of Man. The Word. The Holy Spirit. God the Father. Walking on the waters of the Piave River, holy waters, John the Baptist, Lazarus dead. Lazarus returned to life. He bows his head deeper toward the marble floor and tries to focus on Maria. He closes his eyes and sees her and feels her tender skin, the unrelenting beauty of her touch. Out of this texture and from the depths of his being comes seemingly the most unlikely of thoughts, thoughts about a book he'd been given one day as a young man of fifteen by a traveling bookseller named Avram Daud, who was bringing a cart of books from West to East, heading, he said, to a book bazaar in Baghdad. It was the Mondschein Bible. A line comes to him in the cathedral, head bent, emotions frayed, memory jumbled. *The whole of human history takes place within the seven days of creation, because the one true Creative Act is infinite.* A peculiar book, the Mondschein. Each page, Josef remembers, was divided into two columns. The right-hand column contained the Hebrew text of the Bible, printed in miniscule characters. On the left was an elaborate commentary. In addition, a set of

104

writings followed each book. The central question swirling around the Mondschein Bible was its authorship. Detractors maintain that the whole thing was written by Isaac Mondschein, a man declared insane by the Prussian state and put to death in 1820. Mondschein, on the other hand, states in the preface to the book that the work is a translation of writings by the great luminaries of the Rodrigan Heresy. The central authorial personality that runs at least through much of the textual commentary, Mondschein claims, is that of Enrico Rodriga, a Portuguese Jew who wrote the original in Ladino, which was then translated into German by Mondschein in the first decades of the 19th century. But that's not to say, Daud told him, that all of the commentary is Rodriga's. The 'one true act of creation' line is purportedly the work of Herschel of Ancona, a gnostic interlocutor of Pico della Mirandola and friend of the mysterious Abraham Rodriga, the same Rodriga who later lost himself in Prague amid a maelstrom of controversy.

"For Horak to reach these esoteric heights under the conditions he lived defies reality. What is this but genius! I'm sorry, I know, it's ridiculous to come back to it all the time. I can't help it. It's right there on my tongue. Okay, yes, but back to Josef. He's there in the pew as these thoughts and memories of the Mondschein Bible come flooding back to him with almost vision-like clarity and intensity. Somehow connections start to appear to him between this space—the cathedral—and that former life and then these connections grow and twist together with his present existence and first and foremost with Maria, her eros, her life, her dying. From an intellectual and spiritual point of view, this part of the novel becomes the most important scene for the underground and I'd say the most important scene for humanity, transcending its context completely—as Kafka's cathedral scene transcends, as Dostoyevsky's Grand Inquisitor transcends. Horak released it as a separate story within the novel. Forty or fifty copies were made. Maybe up to a hundred circulated if we count the copies of the copies that seemed to suddenly proliferate through the city. Horak himself has hardly a clue how many were out there and, of course, no precise records exist. The 50-100 comes from Horak's secret police file, a 'document' that can only be described as something between byzantine and post-modern. In terms of the pre-1938 part of the novel, it ranks with the walk from Vítkov to Petřín hill as the most important. To be religious under the regime was in itself tantamount to rebellion—even in fictionalized form—and to express a radical form of Judaism (if we can call Rodriganism by this name) was nearly a capital offense. But this takes us in a different direction. Maybe we'll circle back to it. A couple of years after I took the job to do the translation, after I'd made it through the first reading, I found myself back in Berlin. Florian and I were out at a bar in Kreuzberg, having a rowdy debate about whether the Mondschein Bible was just a figment of Horak's imagination or whether it actually exists or had previously existed. After weighing the evidence, we came to the conclusion that the book is so convincingly portrayed in the text that its reality beyond the novel was utterly out of the question. Two days later, my hangover blissfully over, I made my way to Berlin's Staatsbibliothek. On a whim, I searched the catalog for 'Mondschein,' and found—to my complete shock—an entry for 'Mondschein, Isaac.' I scanned the screen and saw that the book had no digital call number and was marked by the fairly common Berlin bibliographic description: *Kriegsverlust möglich*—possibly destroyed during war. Undaunted by this, I went to the microfilm version of the old card catalog and found the facsimile of the original card. It read, 'Mondschein, Isaac. Bibel.' The publisher was a house called the Rodriga Verlag. Date 1819. Then came a call number. I couldn't believe it. I was so near to it, so close to one of Horak's secrets. Yes, I thought as I sat in the hall of the Stabi, I had found one of Horak's trapdoors, under which was sure to be a warren of dark dens. I put in the order for the book and went to lunch.

"After lunch—and I could barely eat—I returned to the library only to discover that the book couldn't be found. It was apparently missing from the shelf, not that I got any detailed information about how precisely that shelf looked, how large, for example, that gap was. The librarian told me that in all likelihood the book had, indeed, been destroyed or lost during the war. The Hebrew lettering alone would have marked it for destruction. Both Florian and I suspected that Horak had stolen the book. When I eventually felt comfortable enough with Horak to bring it up—and he could be very touchy about these things—he simply ignored my questions. Again, years later during the intermission of a hockey game and with his team comfortable in the lead, I was suddenly inspired to try my luck again. At first, he seemed to ignore me once more and went on to talk about a number of pointless tactical analyses concerning the game and the upcoming period of play. Then, some minutes later, he responded. 'You want to know if the Mondschein Bible exists and if it's what I say it is? Open your eyes, Sy, you've been translating the thing for the past ten years!' Come on! I wanted to shout back above the noise, don't evade, don't confuse, don't obfuscate! I'm not going to play that game. I refuse to play that game, a game in which I'm a pawn on the board. No, no! I composed myself and said rather calmly, 'There's not a single bit of truth in what you just said to me.' 'Truth?' Horak shouted and slammed his beer glass down on the bar so hard that it shattered. 'Truth is what this is all about. And let me tell you this for the first and last time: it's a truth far above what you stubbornly cling to as real!' Angrily, he threw some money on the bar, shoved me violently to the side and left. It was, I think, the only time Horak voluntarily left the viewing of a hockey game before it ended.

"There sat Josef Kostel in the cathedral, sparse congregation around him, the essence of medieval Catholicism pressing down and closing in on him, the dominant figure of Christ looming in the space, thoughts of Mondschein swelling in his mind, pushing out, mixing with, becoming on some level identical with his thoughts of Maria, his lover, his lover who lay dying in that unimaginably empty room deep in the wilderness somewhere—away from him, from his vision and body and paintbrush and soul! He comes to the essential scene for Mondschein and the Rodrigans. There was no way around it. He had to arrive there. The line from Maria's fever to this scene seemed to him at that moment direct and inevitable. Jacob leads his family and flocks away from Laban's camp to return to his native land. On his way, he learns that Esau is up ahead waiting for him and has brought with him four hundred men. There's nothing it can mean, Jacob thinks, but battle. Alone at night on the bank of the Jabbok, the day before the expected fraternal confrontation, Jacob engages in hand-to-hand combat with a mysterious being. From deep in the night until the break of dawn, Jacob and the being wrestle, flight, contest without either of them gaining the upper hand. As dawn breaks, Jacob's hold on his adversary is as tight as ever. The being pleads with Jacob. 'Let me go,' he cries, 'for dawn is breaking.' Jacob senses with whom he's fighting. 'I will not let you go until you bless me.' The being asks for Jacob's name. Jacob tells him. 'Your name,' the being says, 'shall no longer be Jacob, but Israel, for you have striven with beings divine and human and have prevailed.'

"I should point out that the Mondschein Bible was rejected completely by the rabbinical establishment in Berlin and everywhere else the Rodrigans went. It was considered toxic in the countryside where Josef Salomon grew up. From Prague, Warsaw, Vilnius, Berdychiv, Lvov and so on, the bans rained down on both Rodriganism and the book itself. And these bans were but echoes of the two great bans that emerged in the wake of the original Rodrigan Heresy: the initial 1558 ban issued from Venice and the

110

1609 ban decreed from Amsterdam. Book burnings—not uncommon in Germany in these days—followed the banning of Mondschein by Christian authorities. The burning of 1820 after the trial and execution of Isaac Mondschein, the burning of 1831 following the social unrest, and then a burning in 1870 on the eve of unification, which nearly wiped the book from the face of the earth. Among Jews, the book couldn't be burned because it contained the holy text and so there were edicts of interment—resulting in dozens of editions being lost and forgotten.

"The question is how Avram Daud acquired his copy of the book and why on earth would he give it to Josef Salomon on the way to the great Baghdad book bazaar. There's no way of knowing for sure. Much of the story is filtered through Josef's dreamy thoughts in the cathedral and thus veiled by a sort of mental mist. And this history takes a back seat to the more critical thoughts about that wrestling match on the bank of the Jabbok, a tributary stream to the Jordan. The longest and by far most elegant commentary in the Mondschein is found in response to the wrestling match. In the Rodrigan mind, or if you prefer in the wild mind of Isaac Mondschein, that night on the bank of the Jabbok is the turning point of the entire scripture. The commentary starts off in a fairly typical way, walking through the various interpretations of the scene. Some say Jacob was wrestling that night with an angel. Others are more specific, claiming it was the archangel Michael, head of the legions of heaven. Some argue that it was the pesky Satan, the same figure that entices God into tormenting Job. Others maintain that the being was the guardian angel of Jacob's brother Esau. Or was this being, some speculate, Esau himself, who came to Jacob to settle the score between them by grappling one-on-one? Or perhaps there was no being in a material sense. Perhaps the scene was part of an elaborate dream-vision, the likes of which Jacob had already experienced as he fled from his father's house after stealing the birthright from Esau many years before. And if so, this 'wrestling,' some argue, was symbolic of an internal 'wrestling' of Jacob with himself, with his faith in the lord.

" 'No!' cried the Mondscheinian author. The being was not Esau. It was not Esau's guardian angel or Satan or Michael or anything else but God himself. It was God descended to earth to inhabit the form of man, to struggle with the father of His chosen people as men struggle, to fight as flesh and blood. Not Jesus Christ. Goodness, certainly not. This was God. This was El. This was the creator of the universe. God. And Jacob wrestled with God from deep in the night until the break of dawn. And this is the thing: Jacob defeated Him. Yes, this is the key to the whole section, the whole story of Jacob and the subsequent faith. And this key was covered up, denied, buried, burned, or written out. The key is that from the night on the bank of the Jabbok and continuing until this very day God has become the defeated God. The defeat of God, the victory of Jacob over God—this resounds throughout the rest of the biblical text. The most obvious result is that the defeat causes God's withdrawal away from the earth, away from the realm of man. He no longer comes as He came to Jacob at Beth El. He either appears as a symbol—as He appeared to Moses in the burning bush—or He sends His agents. And this defeat and subsequent withdrawal allow history to begin, which is symbolized by the giving of the name Israel to Jacob. Israel implies the historical struggle of the chosen people, a struggle that is initiated by the defeat of God. The defeated God—the withdrawn God. A sulky God, as some detractors derisively say. The story of Moses, of course, tries to restore God's dominance, but it's unsuccessful. The people cannot be tamed even by the demonstration of power against the Egyptians. The law is needed to bind them and a group of enforcers of the law needs to be established. But even here the people continue to stray. God has lost and submits to the idea that the people need a king to control and protect them, that God alone with His law is insufficient. Kings rise to take God's place. They build temples in His name but for their own glory. Can we still love a defeated God, a God of whom we have no fear? Can we still love a God who has withdrawn so incredibly far from us? For Mondschein, the human bridge between the descendants of Jacob and God, those kings and priests, was completely illegitimate—a human construct that had no reciprocity whatsoever. These kings and priests might have usurped earthly power, but they had no access to the vital spirit. These false representatives possessed none of the original creative energy with which God made the world. Instead, they were not *of creation* but *of history*, which resulted from the defeat of God. The legal bridge of the rabbis was a dead-end. It possessed nothing active, nothing activating, nothing that would help a person 'climb the ladder' to heaven step after step, wrung after wrung, upwards, upwards toward that which continued to withdraw. And the lure of another god—Christ—to redeem the whole human enterprise misses the whole point. It was not a matter of sin and thus it could never be a matter of Judgment and redemption. For Mondschein, it was about power. And after Jacob's victory, it became a matter of reconciliation with God. But, as Mondschein quickly points out, reconciliation with a withdrawn God is impossible. He will never manifest Himself again on earth in any form. The idea of a representative, a messiah or savior, is totally rejected here. The withdrawn God would never approve of this. So what does this situation of aspiring for reconciliation with a withdrawn God mean for the believer, for the community of believers, for the Rodrigans and the world? In the Mondscheinian understanding, it meant a striving after the impulse behind the divine act of creation—harmony. And this harmony necessitated the understanding of oneself not as *adam*—as man of flesh—but *adamah*—as ground, earth, soil, dust. The commentary then goes on to describe the period from the eating of the forbidden fruit through the wrestling match on the bank of the Jabbok as one of confrontation, mounting hostility and challenge. Adam and Eve are cast out of the Garden of Eden because God becomes fearful of their power—afraid that if they eat from the tree of life and become immortal they will challenge Him. And then comes the first act of violence, Cain's murder of Abel. This forever breaks any possibility of harmony between God and man because Abel was *adamah* and Cain *adam* and now only *adam*—flesh—remains. And not only has the harmony of God and man been broken, now the harmony of man and man has also been destroyed. This precipitates yet another disintegration, the harmony between man and animal— rent asunder by the first eating of animal flesh. Despite this collapse of the original order so quickly, so fully and fundamentally, God refuses to accept defeat. He attempts to exert His dominance. First comes the flood, which ultimately fails to restore the original harmony. Then the story of Abram/Abraham—where God in His frustration displays His wrath. And so God comes to Jacob to reassert His power. God's defeat is decisive. Jacob ceases to be and Israel is born, political man, disharmonious man. The followers of Israel tread down the path of domination, violence, physical struggle and war. The path of Jacob, on the other hand, is through the dream and up the ladder. The ladder is the symbol of the potential for reconciliation— and I emphasize, as Mondschein emphasizes, potential— and the reestablishment of the original harmony of the one true and infinite creative act: *Let there be light.* God has no will to recreate this harmony, no will to reunite with *adam*, with flesh-man. He could start over by issuing another flood or cataclysm, but the withdrawn God has no interest in that. Rodrigans believe it's the work of the human being to surmount the divine withdrawal. And only through such an overcoming can the original harmony be restored. And when this reconciliation is achieved and harmony is restored, the withdrawn God will again come forth toward the earth, transforming man from *adam* back to *adamah*. Violence ceases as history ceases. The human and the divine again dwell in the eternal now.

"As Kostel sits in the cathedral, he imagines the scene of God again meeting His creation, completing the return to harmony. And what would occur at this moment would be, thought Kostel, a flash of the most majestic beauty possible, a beauty that would shoot directly into every living soul, exciting in the mind of every being the knowledge of the original act of creation: *Let there be light*. To be able to imagine such an impossible flash of beauty, Kostel thinks, to simulate it, to strive after it—this was the meaning of being an artist. Who but an artist, a creator, can conceive of such beauty and through it such harmony? And then, as he bends his head even lower and loses himself completely in these thoughts, he catches a glimpse. Not a full vision. An incredibly miniscule glimpse, limited, fleeting, partial, a flash of form and light together with swirling, bending color. Then one after another the forms and light and colors crystallize into images, appearing and vanishing in a split second. At last, the final image comes, which seems to contain all others within it. Blue. Red. Gray. For the next ten years, Kostel would attempt to translate these images onto canvas, as if this single-minded pursuit would lead directly to reconciliation with God.

"Not long after the visit to the cathedral, Maria died. Her death turned him nearly completely inward and he struggled to reach deeper and deeper imaginative zones. It

117

was by this process that he constructed what he called his color-light forms, compositions ethereal and disturbingly beautiful—disrupting for the viewer, who felt catapulted between pleasure and anxiety. The paintings strove for absolute harmony as a reflection of Mondscheinian perfection. But here Josef discovered something almost unutterable. He found that deep in the realm of harmony, perhaps one or two steps away, lurked its opposite, its Cain. Violence and discord sat at its gates and guarded the transition between mere human harmony and its higher form. Here was the nightmare within the dream—perpetual war of all against all.

"These color-light forms, or simply 'flashes' as Josef called them, first appeared on public view in 1936 in the gallery of Steynberg's greatest rival, Max Zelený, who was connected to the Weisman Gallery in Paris. The Weisman-Zelený connection brought together the biggest show of European surrealism in the 1930s, opening in Paris in June before moving to Prague in November. Four of Kostel's flashes appeared in the show, including his masterpiece, *Blue, Red, Gray.* Kostel, as you can imagine, rejected the idea that the piece was an example of surrealism. In a realm that lacked a 'real,' he said, a surreal was impossible. Critics of the show also questioned the inclusion of the work, calling the flashes representations of an outmoded, decadent style that had little place in the company of symbolically rich, psychoanalytically driven work by his contemporaries. Ideology, politics, consciousness, and sub-consciousness—these were the focal points of the new art. Anything that smacked of metaphysics was considered reactionary. None of the four paintings sold.

"Still, there was no way to deny it—*Blue, Red, Gray* towered over the other works in the show—all other works—at least in the mind of one traveling young journalist named Sidney Keter, a young American who found himself moving through Europe rather aimlessly in the years between the crash of 1929 and the war. Keter is an enigmatic figure, a dreamer, a searcher for something to grasp onto to say, 'This is mine!' He found that something in *Blue, Red, Gray,* an invitation into the Mondscheinian world. It took a year for Keter to track down one of the last remaining copies of the Mondschein Bible, which he found in an old Warsaw bookshop. He set out to translate the book for the first time from German into English, an enormous task, which he accomplished as a squatter in Josef Kostel's studio, doing odd jobs now and then to help Josef pay the bills. And so the next couple of years pass by in an atmosphere of poverty, painting, and discussions of every possible Mondscheinian element. It was just days after Keter finished with the Mondschein that Hitler fol-

lowed the German army into Prague and proclaimed the
end of the republic from Prague Castle.

"Keter fled immediately with the German book and
his English translation. Let me just tell you one thing.
I know you'll find it hard to believe, but it's true. Even
though Sidney Keter is a fictional character, his book exists, or at least it did exist. When he made it back to
New York, Keter got in touch with the Workmen's Circle, which printed the Mondschein Bible in a run of just
twenty copies in 1941. Unfortunately, most of the copies
were destroyed in a warehouse fire on the Lower East Side
a year later. One copy, however, was cataloged in the New
York Public Library. When I investigated it, the librarian actually was able to dig up the record. The book was
checked out on May 10, 1946 by a woman named Esther
Bird and never returned."

I gazed over at Claire, who held her drink just below
her head such that its thin red straw could stick up between her lips. There was no time at this point, precisely
at this point, for a pause to note how her eyes looked
or how subtly her cheekbones sloped to her chin or how
savage those thin lips could be when pursed around that
straw. And there was absolutely no time to think of Gabe
and Elsie and how I sensed, though without proof, that
now and then their thighs pressed together under the table,

how possibly their fingers laced and unlaced, about how their sidelong glances merged and separated, separated hesitantly, uncertainly, despairingly! No time to consider, at least with any depth, how Elsie possessed an Idaishness the likes of which I had never seen before, that I could barely comprehend existed beyond Ida herself, an Ida on stage—and wasn't she always on stage?—an Ida soaring through Gabe's and my collective imagination. No time! No time for the sounds of pretzels, the hum of hockey, the movement of people back and forth and in and out of the Captain's Cabin, between steerage and the deck, in other words, between death and life.

"Under the ubiquitous gaze of the Protectorate," I continued, "Josef was severely compromised. All the dangerous labels—except that of Jew—could be applied to him: surrealist, mystic, avant-gardist, egotist, bohemian, and an example of degenerate urban decadence. On the other hand, Josef was also relatively unknown, insignificant and knew better than most how to recede from view. What follows are some of the most tender pages in the novel. Horak finds a level of startling intimacy in this section of the book that is achingly human. But again, not sentimental. And even when he is sentimental, he's also at the same time not sentimental. It's hard to describe. I can only say that one needs the deftest touch for it. And to translate this—

121

keeping this impossible paradox—only the most artistic mind can do it. I'm not bragging. I'm sorry if it sounds like that, but this is precisely the type of terrain that an academic like Morton from Yale or a hack like Florian could never traverse. Never. Impossible. The story slows here into a harrowing tale of daily banality on a canvas of total oppression, cruelty and fear. There is almost a grinding halt established, sort of like being locked in solitary confinement, dreading the next time someone opens the door, dreading the next page, the next line and yet needing that next page and line to come to relieve the tension and know that the future exists.

"After hundreds of pages full of the love affair with Maria, of Maria's eros and then her drastic illness and death, full of Keter's enthusiasm and energy, of all possible types of discussions of art and life and Rodriganism and Mondschein and the defeated God and the withdrawal, Horak pulls back, and then hones in. The curtain falls. The scene, in a sense, disappears and we find Josef Kostel practically alone on stage. It's a lonely section, lonely not only for Kostel but for the reader, too. And looming beyond the loneliness: Theresienstadt and Buchenwald, Sachsenhausen and Ravensbrück, Auschwitz. And we fear that Kostel will become Salomon again. We fear that the whole constellation of Lalas and Mary Bankes and Mondscheins will be thrown to the flames and turned to ash. Ash. Ash and ash. The fires rise in the distance. The smell of flesh blankets towns and cities. It snows *adam*.

"What can I say about this section? It took me more time to translate these three hundred pages than any other three hundred in the book. Double or triple as long, at least. Slowness defines it. Detail, exacting detail, drives it. Meanings throughout are both material and transcendent. Ten pages, for example, describe Kostel mixing a specific shade of blue, Kostelian blue. Horak is at his most meticulous here. And it is this blue-mixing scene in particular that the state prosecutor in 1980 cited as evidence that Horak was purposefully ignoring the fascist threat and therefore clearly held fascist-capitalist sympathies. Added to this, the prosecutors claimed, was the fact that Horak becomes much more overtly political in the final phase of the book. It was a provocative argument by the state and even rippled through dissident circles. Many dissidents refused to read these pages. Indictments by others were written, condemning Horak for narcissism and escapism. One underground writer claimed that Horak's father had been a Nazi sympathizer—and this indeed was true—and therefore Horak looked west to Germany instead of to the Slavic North, South or East. But whatever the case may be with his father, Horak was about as pure an anti-fascist as has ever existed. His zooming of the lens was a deliberate critique of Nazi mass-thought, fascist mass society. It allows him to preserve his man, Josef Kostel, against all odds.

"And Kostel endures. In the middle of 1940, however, he's put in a very dangerous position. The new governor of the Protectorat, Reinhard Heydrich, wants to have his portrait painted and hung in the anteroom to his office in the Prague Castle. Kostel had painted portraits of quite a few Bohemian industrialists during the lean years of the 1920s and 1930s, one of whom, Karel Lesak, was now cooperating with the Nazis in war production. Lesak recommended Kostel and told Heydrich how satisfied he was with his portrait, which contained not an ounce of contemptible modernity. Heydrich paid a special visit to Lesak's estate in the mountains specifically to view the work and was impressed by the style. When he meets with Kostel, Heydrich compliments his portrait of Lesak, but then he goes on to say that he would need his portrait to be even more magnificent. While Lesak has no eye for these things, he says to Josef, he, Heydrich, could still see traces of effeminate psychologism there, nervous dissipation, degeneracy that ran rampant through the streets of Vienna, Berlin, Munich and just about everywhere else in Europe before 1933. Josef would be tasked with portray-

124

ing the essence of the New Man. As an artist, Heydrich tells him, this is the chance of a lifetime, a higher calling.

"There was no way Josef could turn down the job and remain alive. Mercilessly, Horak keeps us in the sittings with Heydrich for what seems like forever. These scenes are awful, painful, and oppressive in every way. We get detailed descriptions of Heydrich's head, every contour of his face, his chin, mouth, and eyes all emerging from Josef's brush. Ears. Forehead. Impulses to distort and deform seized Josef constantly and he would return to his studio at night and paint gigantic ear-like forms or foreheads that rose out of grassy meadows like denuded mountains—and it could be said that these weeks with Heydrich drove Kostel insane. About halfway through the job, he fell ill and for days was unable to move from bed. Repeated cancellations drew the scrutiny of the secret police, who searched his studio on three occasions. But those ears and foreheads had been burned the instant they were completed and all his older work was now out of Prague boxed in crates and stored in the rafters of a farmhouse barn belonging to a friend of Zelený. There resided *Blue, Red, Gray.* For the first time in his life, Josef started to drink heavily and to fast for no reason other than because he'd lost the desire to eat. Twice he collapsed on the street and was rushed to the doctor, who saw quite clearly that this man was barely alive. But finally, Josef finished. He finished with two straight days of polishing the portrait in his studio during which he succeeded in elevating his version of Heydrich to god-like heights of grandeur. In the end, it was too high, too much. Such an interpretation of Heydrich, with its megalomaniacal aura, could never hang in a public spot; it would immediately arouse the suspicion of Himmler and perhaps even Hitler. Privately, though, Heydrich could cherish it, love it, gaze on it and imagine himself Führer, god, leader of the New Men charged with creating the New World Order. And there he sat in his villa in Paneske-Breschen and imagined himself occupying the throne of Christ, raising now his right hand, now his left to signal the final fate of Man.

"Heydrich didn't have long to enjoy Josef's work. Only weeks after the painting was finished, he was assassinated by the Czech resistance. When Josef learned of the death, he longed to get his hands on the portrait to destroy it. He'd have no opportunity. The whole of Nazi power was on high alert. Retribution was being planned and he could only hope he wouldn't be swept up in it. His access to Heydrich would have made him a suspect in the plot. In any case, the painting was said to be gone from Prague, transported back to Berlin to Heydrich's widow Lina. Perhaps this was the case. Perhaps it did go to Berlin. But in 1946, it resurfaced in Prague and led to Josef's first trial at the hands of the new regime on the charge of being a Nazi collaborator.

"1942. The mechanisms of destruction are churning at full speed. There was no doubt that the Jews were being annihilated. From beneath the shell of Kostel and Mondschein and everything else, Salomon began to stir and come back to life. What does this mean? On the one hand, nothing much. Day-to-day existence didn't change. And yet the past started to explode in his mind every day and then every hour and minute and second. His family, whatever remained of it out there in the depths of the countryside both impossibly far away and within a day's trip, was now gone or would be gone. Destroyed. Josef felt this quake. The tremor entered him and never left. It became part of him, this tremor, this twitch that made it impossible to hold a brush steady. And it grew up from his hand and into his arm and neck and chest and down into his legs. And seizures shook him violently—and perhaps these were the same seizures that shook that young student of the Talmud on the road where he happened to see the bookseller Avram Daud when he fell lifeless in front of his cart. And perhaps these were the seizures that struck Salomon as he pulled himself to safety after managing against impossible odds to cross the Piave River. And perhaps these were the same seizures that could only be quieted by Lala and her opium pipe or Maria and her eros. Time slips as the seizure takes hold. Time goes off the rails as the trains roll. The church bells fall silent and then toll endlessly and noiselessly for the defeated God. Enrico Rodriga had hypothesized that Jacob's defeat of God initiated the first stage of the withdrawal. History, which started then, would have 'Six Great Recessions of the Lord' until he was so distant, so far removed as to be infinitesimal and almost, almost beyond all possible reach, such that the individual person could barely even contemplate the notion of setting off toward Him, let alone the possibility of rapprochement. If, indeed, Rodrigo wrote the essay on Jacob's defeat of God and it wasn't Mondschein or, as many dissidents came to suspect, Keter, then he had identified by around 1520 four of the six recessions. The defeat on the Jabbok instigates the process and sets history in motion. The first moments are not causes of withdrawal but instead indicate its occurrence, one could say that they're its symptoms. The first withdrawal is the enslavement of the people in Egypt. Next, we have the Babylonian destruction of Jerusalem and the Temple and the captivity of the people. The third moment begins with the Roman War in the first century and lasts through the suppression of Bar Kokhba. And finally, as we would expect, the fourth withdrawal was the present one for Rodriga: the expulsion of the Jews from Iberia and the destruction of Spanish Jewry, setting the stage for the broad, lasting and bloody confrontation between the Jews and the Christians of Europe. Two more recessions after 1520. 1942. Was this the fifth or the sixth recession? If it were the sixth, Josef knew from the Mondschein Bible, this would mean it was the so-called Great Recession, a recession that mirrored the sixth day of creation, during which God created man. But since the six recessions mirrored the six days of creation, what would happen on the seventh day, the day of rest? Would God pause in His withdrawal? Would He begin His return? Would He rest? Sleep? Dream? *And God ceased from all the work of creation that he had done.* And on the sixth day God created man in His image.

"I'll admit that Mondschein and Keter are two of my favorite characters. Keter is especially dynamic. He's right there with you, occupying a corner of your mind as he does that far-off corner of Josef's studio. It's strange because this is also the most philosophical part of the book. The ego-driven 1920s and early 1930s give way to a search for something higher—the flight of the soul into distant realms. Foreign realms. Symbol within symbol. But not order. Not determinism! There's no hidden, magic code. Horak's versatility! If anyone needed proof of it, here it is. My god, here it is! The move from Keter to Heydrich to the postwar trials. Fine, admittedly, the three books Horak wrote after 1989 did lack something. The critics are right here. Not that they're bad. How could they be? I'd say they're just less gritty, too graceful in a sense, too literary to reach those Horakian heights. Whatever *Blue, Red, Gray* is rooted in, these three books aren't. They float too high above the material world. And what is this novel rooted in? It's rooted in the precise spot where the body and soul meet. Only Horak could search out this spot, till it, cultivate it, and spend years transforming this rocky ground into arable, fecund soil. Here it is—imagine that manuscript, piled as high as a mountain. It's looming above you like some distant peak, ancient and grandiose and mysterious and frightening and sublime. Horak. Jan Horak. A name—no. A body—no. A symbol. God help us! God help us if I get too drunk to finish this. If I can't finish this, I can't finish anything, including life.

"It was 1988. The novel was finally finished. The concluding section, the second trial of Josef Kostel as an enemy of the state, is done. I'll come back to it in a minute. It's an incredible piece. Not that I need to say it. You know by now. You know it. Feel it. All of you. Another novel within the novel. Yet another. A more timid writer would have just released the thing in four or five or six

130

parts. Not Horak. Its fragmentation was its whole. 1988. The manuscript in its Promethean totality is typed for the first time. I mean, the first time all at once. In some sense, dozens or even hundreds of 'complete' copies were out there, but in pieces. Maybe someone had managed to stitch one together, but such hoarding of pages—and especially of this book—went against dissident ethics. You read and you passed the pages on. The hoarder was by definition suspect. To hoard gave one the means to betray, to break the chain of trust. No chain. Ha! The thread of trust, so thin and delicate. It was a thread that was almost impossible not to break. It's 1988. The last chapters had been done for almost a year by now. Some thirteen months passed between the final writing and the production of the first typed copy. Alena did the whole thing on an old typewriter. They had no access to a copy machine. To copy anything was to risk its loss. You might wonder whether Horak cared about loss, seeing as he was seemingly unconcerned about the distribution process. He's still unconcerned and given the history of the last two and a half decades, he's more reluctant than ever to play by the rules. Horak despises rules of any kind.

"Things were smoldering in the underground. Word was coming from across the border in Poland that the mood was shifting decisively. The grip of the regime was loosening. I mean, we know the story from the highest levels—Gorbachev, Reagan, Thatcher, Kohl—but I'm not talking about any of that. I'm talking about something much more important and less tangible—the spirit of the people, the collective will of the people to elevate themselves, to rise, to unchain themselves from oppression. A group of dissident exiles with members in Paris, London and Toronto calls for Horak's book. Its moral force, they tell him through the underground, could be a decisive blow. Horak decides to take the risk. Plans start to develop to get the typed copy out of Czechoslovakia, to print it by the thousands, and to secret the printed copies back into the country. A moral challenge, they were calling it, a spark to light the national fire, the fire for individual freedom, for individual integrity, for control over one's life, history, and future. To rock the legitimacy of the regime, already teetering on the edge of collapse.

"Now picture the scene," I said and actually rose to my feet at this point while the others at the table—Gabe, Elsie, Claire—peered up at me in drunken disbelief. I remained standing until the end. "Horak is taken north by car. Makes four transfers to try to throw off the secret police, who, it turns out, were actually on his tail. I've seen the records myself. Amazing stuff. The plan: Horak is taken to a lodge in the mountains some twenty kilometers by foot from the summit of Sněžka, the highest mountain in the country. There, in the dusk, he sets out into the Krkonoše Mountains, heading for Sněžka. The border between Czechoslovakia and Poland runs right through Sněžka's summit. On the Polish side stands the small Chapel of Saint Lawrence, built in the middle of the 17th century. It was in the chapel that Horak's contact waited, a man charged with taking and delivering the manuscript to the next link on the chain in Warsaw. There, in Warsaw, it would change hands again and be taken to Gdansk, where another man—and this is said to have been my editor Carl Glaser, the Chief—posing as a member of the Swedish merchant marine, would transport the book to Stockholm and thus to the free world. The story, of course, is hearsay. Carl and Horak wouldn't talk about it. For a long time, I believed that this Polish 'priest' in the Chapel of Saint Lawrence was none other than Carl Glaser, though my faith in this was shaken by a disturbing tale about that meeting that Horak told me while drunk following the gold metal game of the 2005 hockey world championship, which the Czechs won (thank god!) 3-0 over Canada.

"The Czech edition was printed immediately in Toronto. By the end of January 1989, copies began to flow back into Czechoslovakia. Some months later there

133

was a hum, an almost audible tension, produced as the book made its way through Prague society—like sugar moving through the blood. During the summer of 1989, it seemed like half of Prague was somehow reading the book, despite there being probably less than a thousand copies altogether in the country. As the tension built, as the hum grew into a din, an alarm, the question rippling through the underground was whether—or when—the regime would come down on Horak. Would he be arrested? Would he be tried? In July, rumors started to fly that Horak had been arrested. At the same time, events in Poland were moving. The first walls were falling hard and fast. Even the rumors that Horak was under arrest started to catalyze something larger than the underground. Tension. The tension was unbearable by the end of the month, so unbearable that the newspapers printed an article claiming (correctly) that Horak was not in jail. Imagine! It must have been an absolute first for the communist government. It was Horak's force. The force of *Blue, Red, Gray*.

"We can't get too far into that. Needless to say the article confounded people and caused people to think the exact opposite. It's been said that this article was the ultimate symbol of the dying of the regime. Not the death. The dying. The near death. The drying up—the Raven. There

134

was a black and white picture of Horak in the article. He's wearing a pair of jeans with a belt with a large buckle. He's got on a sort of striped polo shirt with a white collar. His face is unshaven, his hair unkempt. He's on the sidewalk looking down at someone or something in the distance in Rieger Park. Tall, lean—a handsome man. He seems transformed here, transformed into ethos or even demos by a greatness incomprehensible to us in the West, a greatness by dint of his total creation, his total world or total vision, so total that by the end of it there was no longer room for that other world, that illegitimate sham-reality of communist Europe, a world of corruption, ignorance, violence, and fear.

"The Chapel of Saint Lawrence. A man with no name. No identity. Dressed as a priest. Perhaps he was a priest. In any case, he had the leather binding from a 17th century Latin Bible ready to wrap the book. Did Horak, does Horak, believe in God? Does he believe in the defeated God? Copies of Mondschein start appearing in Horak's reality. In D.C., in Berlin, in Paris. Destroyed. Destroyed. Destroyed by the enemies of the Rodrigan faith. The man. Or were there two men—the dark and the light, the good and the evil? Some think there was a wrestling match with the first man, an agent of the KGB. Some think that Horak prevailed after a night of fierce struggle. A few have told

135

me that they think Horak might have killed this man and that around dawn the second man arrived—perhaps Carl Glaser—in clerical clothing and with that Bible binding in hand.

"Whatever the truth may be, Horak came down from the mountain, returned to Prague, and fell horribly sick. He was nervous, depressed. The rumors about his arrest seemed plausible because for a long time after this, and still in the summer of 1989, he was barely leaving home. The photograph of him standing above Rieger Park was a fake. The image of Horak was of three years earlier and was taken by a friend (apparently a regime informant) on a day trip to Brno. The picture was then superimposed onto another image of the scene. There is no doubt about it. In the photo, Horak is wearing a cheap broad-faced silver-plated watch. But this was precisely the watch he lost during that night on Sněžka! One would think that the secret police would have known this. One would think that they would have noted down, 'Horak returns without his watch.' But nothing of the sort is found in the file, despite the existence of thousands upon thousands of much less significant details.

"Why did Horak have this breakdown? And was this the beginning of what might be described as a long, slow, total breakdown of a great man? The truth is that Horak never fully recovered. He gradually slipped away into chronic depression, alcoholism and insignificance. The writings after the Velvet Revolution lack that counterforce that animates the whole of *Blue, Red, Gray* and large sections of *Rain, Rain*. This counterforce elevated the work above the ground. Like the sun, the work rose, set, and rose again each day. Like the moon, the work waxed to fullness and thus reflected as much as possible the primary source of light. After another beer, I might even admit to believing that at its summit, the novel, itself a mountain, reflects the original source of creative genius—the rising of the wind from the deep, the molding of form by the wind. And yes, of course, the raven was Noah's symbol of the divine wind—the raven's sending forth Noah's attempt to reenact, to represent, the creation of the world."

I paused here and took a long drink, finishing the beer in front of me. Chuck, who seemed also to be half following my story, immediately signaled to me to check if I wanted another round. I most certainly did—and signaled back with a circular twirl of my index finger to indicate that he should refresh all the drinks at the table. Chuck immediately started to arrange glasses and bottles. I closed my eyes and found my way back to Josef Kostel.

"The first trial of Josef Kostel revolved around the question of whether he was a willing collaborator with the

Nazis, whether he had voluntarily agreed to paint the portrait of Heydrich. The process involved a team of experts, who came to Josef's studio, interviewed him and examined his work. They talked to everyone who knew Josef and who had remained in Prague—many were dead or gone, like Steynberg and Keter. The case was settled in a matter of days. There was no evidence of willing association with Heydrich and plenty to point to at least internal resistance to the Nazi regime. Josef, the final report read, had been forced to do the painting, which he considered an odious task. The case was dropped. In those immediate post-war days, there were plenty of big fish to fry. This event could barely be called a trial. It was part of the general wave of retribution sweeping over the country.

"The grounds for the next trial seemed to Josef just as outlandish. By then the coup had taken place and the communists were in charge. Kostel was identified as an enemy of the state and of the Czech and Slovak people and as an agent of capitalism and foreign propaganda. The indictment centered on a single painting: *Blue, Red, Gray.*

"The second trial—the only real trial—became another and the final novel-in-the-novel. It reads like something between Beckett and Arthur Koestler, a masterpiece of tragic farce. It is undoubtedly the most devastating depiction of the postwar communist system outside of

Solzhenitsyn. Early sections of this final part of the novel, traceable back to the late 1970s—so around the time of the Charter 77 or Havel's 'Power of the Powerless'— resulted in multiple arrests of Horak and altogether a couple of hard years in prison. The regime sought to locate and destroy all copies of these chapters, a search that compromised the existence of the entirety of the novel. We know from the secret police file that in 1982 an order was handed down that called for 'the eradication of all work by Jan Horak.' By this time, there were simply too many copies out there for this to be possible, too many places to hide them, and not enough fear among the people. The regime itself was too slow, bumbling, and uncreative to accomplish such a task. And the original copy—Horak's handwritten notebooks? Nobody knows. Nobody besides Horak and Alena has ever seen them, including me!

"Again a panel of experts. Art historians from around the country—newly promoted to chair their respective university departments in Prague, Brno, and Bratislava. The purpose of this team was to present arguments to substantiate the government's claim that *Blue, Red, Gray* was anti-communist art, that it was a disguised piece of capitalist propaganda meant to promote individuality, to attack collectivity, and to undermine the new progressive workers' state. By then, 1950, the Czech academy had been twice purged, once in 1946 and then again (and in Stalinist fashion) in 1949. The three experts, in great Horakian style, are given without last names: Tomaš J., Kašpar P., and Pavel C. Each of the three experts got a full day to present his analysis. They divided the days by color. J. took blue, P. red, and C. gray.

"Blue. There's no denying it, J. says, the blue represents the very essence of liberalism. The blue of Kostel's painting is the blue of the French Revolution, the blue of American freedom fighters against the British, the blue of Napoleon's *Grande Armée* on the march, the blue of the Union North. Moreover, says J., it's the blue of the high seas, of British imperialism, the blue of commerce and trade, the blue of the rise of banking in the Low Countries and England, the blue of empire. Blue, he says, like all color has materiality, but it also has symbolic meaning and thus is an essential part of what Marx would call the superstructure. Color becomes part of the obfuscating screen, denying the worker his or her clear vision of egalitarian, anti-individualistic society. The blue, J. testifies, dominates the canvas, pushing the red to the periphery, just as the bourgeoisie marginalize the workers. And the spot of red toward the middle, it's surrounded on all sides by blue, just as the bourgeoisie imprison the workers in the status of wage-laborer, shackled by debt, a slave to the clock, the machinery of capitalism

140

churning around the worker, swallowing him, devouring him. The blue, J. says, encroaches. It moves ever outward, just as liberalism, according to Lenin, necessarily leads to imperialism. In Czechoslovakia, argues J., blueness, this fetishization of the blue, is doubly pernicious. It presents a Utopian, historicist understanding of the years of the republic, totally failing to capture its weakness, corruption and desire—yes, desire!—to be dominated by fascist capitalism. The blue and, as C. will discuss, the gray almost merge in places, becoming a smoky, inky charcoal, just as the Czech bourgeois nation became one with Nazi fascism. Yes, J. says, it's the fate and even the goal of bourgeois power to give itself over, to prostrate itself before, fascist tyranny. By way of historical entropy, says J., blue transforms into gray, gray becomes the anarcho-fascist black, the only color that is fully able to eradicate all traces of communist red.

"Kašpar P. An older man. A sycophant. He has no originality, nothing of J.'s intelligence. He got his position as chairman of the art history department in Prague after two decades of mediocrity and a languishing career as a scholar of late medieval icon painting, of course taking a materialist view, which immediately catapulted him to the top of the field after the war. Bald, plump, pale—it seemed like P. survived off dumplings, cabbage and the occasional chunk of meat. It was a diet that contributed much to his soft rotundity and sour odor. The one attribute that had survived undiminished since youth, miraculously, was his full set of large, brilliant teeth, which he often displayed by purposefully retracting his lips as far as they would go during pauses in his elocution. But P. didn't need genius to accomplish his goal. He was the transition man, taking the well-constructed case from J., moving it forward a little bit, and then handing it off to the C. The main thrust of P.'s testimony was the beleaguered position of red in the painting. Red. The red was under siege, said P., by the imperial blue and the haunting, creeping gray. Despite that, and in spite of Kostel's intent, the red was heroically holding its own. Only the most grotesque perversion of historical materialism was trying to blot it out. And this element, this besieged red, was the painting's chief weakness. It completely alienated the communist spectator, making it both useless and dangerous and a potential catalyst of counterrevolutionary aspirations. For those still infected by pre-revolutionary notions of beauty, P. said, the painting was comprehensible but disgusting, its whole composition undermined by the unjustifiable marginalization of red. What's more, according to P., the red seems destined to break the chains, and if this were to happen it would mean the complete annihilation of the work!

"C. was an aesthete, an academic of the highest order. An intellectual. A purist. A dogmatist. He pursued the truth, as he saw it, at all costs, which had earned him a professorship in Bratislava before the war, before the Nazis came and sent him to Buchenwald and then from there to the underground slave labor camps of Dora-Mittelbau.

"Gray. C. knew gray. His life had been dominated by gray. It was the dusty color of hard, driving labor. Stone ground into powder, powder into dust, the dust driven day after day into the skin. The skin turned gray from dust and starvation and anguish and hopelessness. From despair. From being surrounded for years by death. What is this creeping grayness in the painting? For sure, C. begins, it implies, as J. said, an anarcho-fascism with a goal of the snuffing out of the working class, choking it as pollution chokes the proletariat in London, Manchester, Lyon, and Pittsburgh. So gray is also pollution. And it's also pessimism in the form of Thanatos, the death drive, lifted from the gloomy pages of Freud's *Civilization and Its Discontents*—one of the most vicious attacks on the notion of the 'communal' to ever flow from a pen. And so the gray here is also rank bourgeois Freudianism, a Spenglerism infected by an aesthetic preference for the feminine over the masculine, the homosexual over the normal. And this all meant a fundamental opposition, a struggle of life and death, between red and gray. That the red is shown perversely in retreat points to the depths of Kostel's counter-revolutionary agenda.

"Gray. How many times does C. say the word gray? Hundreds. Over and over, he utters it to devastating effectiveness. And then comes the conclusion. Beyond the obvious meanings, C. announces at the end of his long testimony, is a hidden, coded meaning, which truly elevates the painting to the status of a dangerous, virulent, contagious bacteriological weapon of enemy propaganda. The gray, in essence, is the entire power structure of International Trotskyism. The intent of this force is as it has always been—the destruction of the workers' state and the continued enslavement of the worker. The painting contains clear proof of this Trotskyism. Nothing could be clearer. The politics of the painting—liberal Trotskyite. The central thrust of the painting—the blue transforming into a creeping grayness—a smoky fog meant to blind the worker. Isn't this precisely why the gray seems to overtake the red at every spot? The gray comes as Trotsky's God comes, as Jehovah comes, to dilute the struggle, to distract the worker from the march of historical materialism, to lull the worker into the opium haze of false faith. It was Karl Marx's greatest triumph, C. maintains, to have overcome his own faith, to have thrown it off in order to embark on climbing the mountain of economic understanding, on the summit of which he found the core principles of *Das Kapital*. See Marx, standing atop that peak, gazing down on the villages in the valley. They swarm with evil—the money-lenders, the tyrannical inn- and tavern-keepers, parasitical distillers, diabolical master craftsmen, and those spinners of ideological spider webs: the rabbis, Talmudists, and bearded mystics. And beyond those villages, Marx gazes on the cities—the bankers, the war-profiteers, the dandyish lawyers and doctors and intellectuals of all sorts, the managers and sort-handed clerks, the Freemasons and the *maskilim*. And below the belching smokestacks of the factories sit the industrialists in their plush offices and country estates, which once belonged to Lords and Junkers and Boyars. And the whole spirit of the land—from the tiniest village to the new sprawling metropolis—the animate force of capitalism: usury.

"The judge in 1946, C. says, found that Josef Kostel had been wrongly charged with collaboration with the Nazis. He was no doubt correct. But while his Trotskyism prevented his sympathy with the Hitlerites, it's the root cause of his past and current aggression toward the worker and his greatest achievement, the workers' state.

"With that, the prosecution finished and Josef returned to his cell. On some level, his defense was clear. His painting had nothing at all to do with politics. It was about Mondschein and the defeated God and the withdrawals and the harmony and reconciliation. But how could any of it stand up against Marx and the workers' state? Against Lenin and capitalist imperialism? Against Stalin and the great purge? A vague longing overtook him for Keter to return to argue the case for him. Keter could explain everything with his fantastic energy, the wrestling match on the bank of the Jabbok, Jacob's victory, the six great recessions corresponding to the six days of creation, the seventh day, the mystery of the seventh movement of the defeated God, the connection between the ultimate harmony and his color flashes. The true meaning of *Blue, Red, Gray.* Keter could do this. Keter must do this! And yet Keter had vanished without a trace.

"The next day, Josef enters the courtroom and stands before the judge. The judge prompts him to begin. Josef's lawyer, a state-appointed hack, rises and speaks for about five minutes. He says that though the art might be degenerate and reflective of bourgeois reactionism (there was little way to deny it), it was also harmless. Almost nobody had seen the work and it hadn't been publicly displayed once after the formation of the workers' state. The lawyer says that Josef has no intentions of creating additional work in a similar style and with his clear mastery of

146

a variety of artistic forms he could be useful to the state, a usefulness that would be completely wasted if he found himself in prison or worse. Finally, the lawyer claims that Josef is not a Trotskyite, that any political message that appears in the work was quite accidental, a product more of the times than of the man. In this new context of the workers' state, the lawyer says, there will be new, corresponding outcomes in Josef's art. The lawyer stops. Despite its brevity, Josef finds himself quite satisfied by the defense, despite having no intention of shifting his style to match the regime's desires. When the judge asks Josef if he has anything else to add, he shakes his head and remains silent. Again, the judge asks, telling him that this is his only chance to provide his perspective for the official record. Again, Josef remains silent, this time dropping his gaze from the judge to the floor.

"The following day the judge pronounces Josef guilty of producing propaganda aimed at undermining the morale of the worker. Kostel, the verdict read, was banned from producing and displaying any form of art. He was prohibited from possessing the tools that belonged to the artist's craft—paintbrushes, etching tools, canvas and so on. All the work he had stored in his studio and anywhere else was to be surrendered immediately to the police to be destroyed. Needless to say, the verdict added, if Kostel were caught selling art on the black market, this would be deemed a capital offense, because it would combine the crime of being an agent of foreign propaganda with a high economic crime. Finally, because his work as an artist was now illegal, Kostel would have to be made useful to the state and thus socially rehabilitated through labor. The judge assigned him to a ten-year term in the steel mills of Ostrava, the position to begin in one month. Failure to report for work in Ostrava would result in immediate imprisonment for the same period—ten years. 'It's the state's duty,' the judge tells Josef, 'to inoculate society against this infectious individualism before it can enter the social bloodstream. And there is no better method for this, Josef Kostel, than honest hard labor with your hands.'

"The destruction of his studio happens before he makes it home. Nothing remains of his work. The tools he'd acquired in Italy are gone. It was time, Josef thought, to disappear again, to vanish as Salomon had vanished. But where to go? And how would he escape now that his every move was being watched by police, neighbors, by anonymous people in the street, by everyone? Still, it was time to vanish. It was time for his retreat. He had wrestled with the state and lost decisively. Blue, Red, Gray—this had been his call out into that indescribable realm. Into the furnace in the basement of police headquarters it went!

Incinerated. And in the darkness that followed the destruction, a figure moved through the streets of Prague and then out into the countryside. At the edge of the forest, he vanishes. At first, we think we can follow his form as it weaves between the trees. Then not anymore. No longer. Nothing. Nothing exists but the traces of memory of a life that itself quite possibly never was, a body more water than earth, more air than fire. That's how the book ends. That's how I end it. My god, could it be that I end it! That an end is possible? I doubt it. I do. I doubt the whole thing every time I close my eyes."

I stopped and fell back down into my seat. As if someone had flicked a switch, the noise from the bar came rushing into my consciousness and I realized I had perceived complete silence while I'd spoken. While I was telling the story, the Captain's Cabin seemed to have reached its peak hour. Nearly every chair was occupied. Even Elsie's former position at the bar had been overtaken. A rather pear-shaped man with bushy sideburns, an unflatteringly tight brown suit, and rectangular glasses sat beside Paul's jacket with a martini glass in one hand and his phone in the other. Paul had not returned.

"You've got to be kidding me!" a voice rang out. It was Morgan, who, I saw, had turned away from the television in disgust, his non-beer-holding hand entangled in his thick brown hair. The divergence of my attention seemed to loosen the grip of my story on the table. Claire began to fuss with the strap of her bag, which hung on the back of her chair, in order, I assume, to indicate imminent departure. Elsie kept her eyes trained on Gabe, waiting for his response. Gabe continued to stare at me for a minute or two and then glanced down at his watch. I followed his eyes and saw that it was now shortly after 11pm. I slumped down into my chair and sipped my beer. The telling had exhausted me and my stomach churned from hunger. Detached from any particular goal, my mind started to spin. I focused on steadying it, on steadying myself. On some level, I felt the need to try to steady myself in a deeper—a fundamental—way and that if I didn't do it, didn't concentrate with all my force, I would collapse completely in a heap like a marathon runner right after reaching the end line.

"I really need a smoke after that," said Elsie, still staring over at Gabe. "Would anyone like to join me?"

Claire and I quickly turned down the offer. For a few moments, Gabe didn't respond. He seemed completely lost in thought, and I wondered at that moment how much of the story he had actually heard. His eyes were narrow and focused on me—a look that could have meant a number of things, ranging from respect and admiration on the one hand to doubt and suspicion on the other. Suspicion of what? Dissimulation. Deception. There was no purpose or way for me to confront this look—whatever look it was. I quickly diverted my eyes.

"Why not," said Gabe and slowly rose to his feet.

They put on their jackets and left. Claire and I remained at the table. Another round of drinks appeared.

"Your father must be very proud of the work you're doing," she said as she sipped her newly arrived drink through its thin red straw. I know she meant it as ordinary conversational fodder, but the comment sent a convulsion through my tired, hungry and intoxicated body. Maybe it was the alcohol or the emptying out of my verbal capacity, the purgation of the story all at once like that for the first time in seventeen years, but I suddenly felt incredibly raw.

"That's a tricky one, very tricky. I'm not sure I can say he's proud of me. At some point, five or six years ago, I think, I called and asked him for some money. It must've been in one of my periods of acute shortage. The whole thing with Horak has been disastrous for me from a financial point of view. I hated doing it, but I needed a boost to see me through to the end. That's what I told him. I said I needed one final push, one last big push and it would be over. The book would be done. Do you know what he told me? He said, 'There will never be an end.' And then he

151

said that I was wasting my life on this 'so-called Horak.' So-called! I slammed down the phone. It was still one of those old slammable types. But he did send me some money, a stack of traveler's checks with no accompanying note."

"I don't know your father very well, but I have a hard time imagining him saying those things. He seems so gentle and kind."

"Maybe you're right," I said and shook my head. I took a long drink and continued. "When it comes to my father, I've lost perspective. Maybe he didn't say it. I was struggling at the time. But I think he said it. It's hard to know with him, it's hard to know with me."

"Are you going to visit him while you're here?"

"My parents live most of the year in West Palm Beach. I don't think I'll make it down there. Not now. It's not the right time. I need to get back to Prague as soon as possible to finish the book. It's at the end. It's one step away. My brother Henry thinks I'm too self-absorbed and obsessed with this Horak project to care about anything else. He's partially right, I guess, about most of it. But he's still missing the fundamental point."

"And what's that?"

"I'm not sure. I know there's a fundamental point and I'm pretty confident Henry's missing it. I've always thought, or sensed, that though Henry knew everything else, he didn't know that which was most essential. Not that I know it. No, of course not. But I could know it. And if I did know it, I'd probably be on the first flight down to West Palm Beach."

"I wish I was on the first flight out of here—to anywhere. My interview's at 9am and I'm completely drunk. This is the only call-back I got."

"If this storm continues, assuming there's really a storm up there as everyone says, there's a good chance the whole thing will be postponed. We should stay down here and pray to the snow god."

"Enough god for one night. I'm starting to doubt my atheism. I don't think I've heard that much about god since church with my grandmother when I was a kid. And those aren't the most pleasant memories."

"How old are you, Claire?"

"Thirty-one, thanks for reminding me. Maybe I should've taken that cigarette. I suddenly have the urge to smoke."

She shifted in her chair and then leaned back with her arms stretched out over her head, creating a pleasing and momentary arching shape. She crossed, uncrossed and then recrossed her legs, which were covered in dark gray stockings.

If we take 1997 as the obvious starting point, I'd had five major relationships and some additional minor ones in my years in Prague. The majors included Meg, the Canadian, in some sense a Claire-like figure, though much more deceitful, cunning and horrible. Meg took from me and then made me suffer, even attempting at one point to seduce Horak, fortunately unsuccessfully, while I was in the kitchen preparing his post-pub black coffee. So I'll leave her out—and enough of her already! If I could dissect her from my memory, I would do it in a second. In any case, my first serious relationship after Ida left Berlin was with Irena, a sociology student who also worked as a waitress in a cheap but still somewhat elegant Czech restaurant I frequented and where I ate steak at least once per week. She was nineteen when we met and the whole thing had little chance to make it very far. It had spirit—a lot of sex, a lot of drinking, some fantastic times in Budapest and Vienna, even a return trip (my first) to Berlin, where she ended up sleeping with Florian while I was out at the library for a day of work on *Blue, Red, Gray.* That was that. I tried to love Irena like I thought I loved Ida; that is, I wanted to totally surrender every part of my being to her. Being nineteen and who she was, she was unprepared to take on this poisonous gift, though she would attempt to do it for a few months at a time only to back out suddenly and utterly. She must have viewed Florian as a way out after two unbelievably intense years of near constant emotional upheaval—at least for me. In the meantime, I really started to learn Czech. In some ways Irena's Czech was the closest to Horak's that I've ever heard. Maybe that was what it was about in the end. I was passionately in love with her language, her words, and the cadences of her breath. And I wanted to immerse myself in it, to swim in it.

The next relationship was tamer, too tame. I met Filipa in Big Apple Books, an English-language bookshop with an attached café/bar. Big Apple was the second home to a generation of ex-pats—those deep into James Joyce and those who just drowned themselves in drink. Filipa was uncomplicated. The chief trait that attracted me to her was that she wasn't Irena. And she wasn't Ida Fields. But her unIdaishness was ultimately not enough. I sensed that she was with me for a similar reason, a respite from something more fulfilling but also destructive, something much more real. We bored each other and broke up without hard feelings after some years. I hardly remember how long it lasted. But she did introduce me to a few important things. She taught me, for example, how to identify edible mushrooms—key to my translation. She took me into the Czech countryside and through her I came to appreciate its quiet, lazy beauty. Most importantly, it was with Filipa that I first made the trip north to the Krkonoše Mountains to climb Sněžka. It was with her, Filipa, that I first stood in the Chapel of St. Lawrence and breathed that rarefied air. This was before I knew anything at all about Horak's encounter in the chapel that night! Even. Boring. Polite. A prelude to Meg. Yes, Meg came next. For many years, I've tried to get rid of the hatred I have for her. Without fail, her odiousness vitiates my best intentions and strongest will. But I refuse to talk about her here, to let her in here. She tried to undermine and destroy me, but I eventually won out and she retreated. It was a victory that came at incredible cost.

Following the Meg debacle, I had a short but serious affair with Julia, an Italian historian. Julia was a woman of broad intellect and savage beauty, much too much of the latter for me. For her, I was a distraction from her long days of archival research. She was in Prague for about ten months hunting for the papers of the Jewish convert to Rodriganism Abraham Rodriga. Julia was investigating the so-called 'second path thesis,' the idea that Rodriganism didn't originate in Iberia in response to inquisition and expulsion but first appeared in southern Italy in the ninth century amid a sect of reclusive mystics before moving north. It was Abraham Rodriga, so the theory goes, who, generations later, took the faith to a Bohemia still in the grip of the Hussite challenge. From there, it moved into Poland and the Germanic lands, finding strong footholds only in Amsterdam in the 17th century and Berlin in the 18th. Abraham Rodriga's papers, of course, were the key to the puzzle, to many puzzles, including the ultimate question—a question that drove Julia to the point of utter exhaustion and eventual mental and emotional paralysis: the authorship of the Mondschein Bible.

She left Prague empty-handed. I imagine in some ways I symbolized or embodied her failure, considering that I made promises to find books and documents that I was reasonably sure never existed. But they were pledges of love, of desire, attempts to conquer the world, which included bending history to my will in order to satisfy Julia's spiritual and physical longings. For a time at the end of her stay in Prague, I would've given up everything to follow her back to Rome. I would even have left *Blue, Red, Gray* unfinished. But that, like so much else, was a fantasy. Never for a second did Julia consider it.

It took a long time to recover from Julia's departure—years, in fact, hard years, during which I'll admit I kept replaying those three months in 1997. Gray winter months in Berlin with Ida, early spring—a disaster of a season. Finally, after all those years, I was with Ida Fields. It didn't help that there was a pause in the work with Horak. The first draft was done. Carl had it read in a matter of weeks and sent back a healthy set of comments. I felt ready to take them on, but Horak was exhausted and soon fell ill, needing eventually to leave Prague to spend close to a year, the first of many more to come, at the Grünhofberg, a facility that's something between an old-fashioned neurasthenia clinic and an alcohol rehab center. His absence left me without purpose. There was no way I could work without him.

What year was Horak's first retreat into the Grünhofberg? What do years matter? As I sit here with these measly twenty pages next to me, I laugh at years and days and months and dates and seconds. I laugh at time! Time! My god, those three months in 1997 contained more time than my entire life before and after. Time! Those eight hours in that basement bar with Gabe—how many lifetimes do they represent? Our constant measuring, our sorry attempt to ascribe value, what's this but the ultimate blasphemy. God created all time—all history—in just six days. One day, no, one second of perceived time is an infinite extension of one creative act. And how many such infinite moments happened during those three months in 1997? Those months with Ida, beginning in the abandoned hall of the closed-down Tempelhof airport—she the only passenger to disembark from that non-existent plane. With those words, "There you are." And ending— when? Later. Later. With an evacuation from Zoo Station.

Penelope. Pepi. She was the last and greatest of my Prague lovers. We met under Filipa's eyes at a night of literary readings at the Big Apple café and bar while Horak was again recuperating at the Grünhofberg. Pepi is a Czech poet and an American friend of hers, Sally Patton, had translated a half dozen of her poems into English for the event. After the reading, I saw her at the bar having a drink by herself. Sally (whom I knew quite well) was off talking to some other people. I approached her and, naturally, introduced myself as the translator of Horak's *Blue, Red, Gray*. She said: is that right? Yes, I said, the second draft is done and we've just started on the third. She wanted to know what I thought of the poems. It was hard to say, I said, having heard only the translations. And what did I think of those? Though I haven't seen the originals, I told her, my immediate impression was that Sally hadn't gotten the tone or mood quite right. But the bigger issue, I said, was that Sally had missed the organic rhythm of the work. Each poet, I said, has a different rhythm, and it seemed to me that Sally either transplanted a rhythm from one poet to another or she just flattened the contours of all poetry into her own rather boring and totally unpoetic form. She's a middle manager, I told her after I ordered my drink, or a clerk posing as a translator of poetry. Soon Sally will return to the U.S. and start working on marketing campaigns for eyeliner or lip-gloss or something like that. I guess you didn't like the work, Pepi said. "I found it atrocious," I blurted out. We had great sex that night and in the calm, candle-lit afterglow in her hideous Soviet-era apartment so far from any part of Prague I'd ever seen (and I'd seen it all by that time) she read me her real work in Czech. Pepi. My Pepi. Her father had been an active party member, an accountant who kept the books for a chemical factory in the Prague suburbs. Her grandfather had been a member of the Czech resistance against the Nazis and had been captured and killed as retribution for the Heydrich assassination. Her grandmother became an informer for the secret police until she herself was informed on in the late 1950s. Her brother Štěpán played cello in the Prague Symphony Orchestra. Her mother was a chronic depressive, was institutionalized in the early 1990s and died of cancer in 1995. Her other set of grandparents passed away some few years before we met and left her the apartment in that nearly uninhabitable part of the city.

Pepi was like a tender wildflower growing in some post-apocalyptic zone. Her delicate beauty, her fragility, made me want her in a way I'd never experienced before. Her family had been destroyed by history, leaving her an orphan of history's crime. And so she floated out there, that orphan, that forgotten child. She was complex, dynamic, and full of life—a fullness only matched by that of Jan Horak at the height of either his drunkenness or his sobriety, right before, that is, he fell into violent, tempestuous, and vomitous incomprehensibility. In a battle between creative gods, Pepi could stand toe-to-toe with Horak, though ultimately Horak (like Jacob on the Jabbok) would prevail. And did. He did prevail. I couldn't handle both of them once Horak returned from his stay at the Grünhofberg. But the process of displacing Pepi—of pulling her out of my life—took years and a hell of a lot of regret. Not that it was only me doing the pulling and not that I only pulled. No. I pushed and pulled. She would disappear for weeks at a time and then show up at my small apartment and, Lalaesque, barely leave for months. At one point, I demanded that she get rid of Sally and have me translate her work. Our long, late nights of work together produced some real flashes of brilliance—a beam of radiance to cut through Prague's gray, foggy life. An example:

Hereness
    Doesn't exist.
There.

There is a cat slinking through the garden at night to the
    compost heap.
Night.
    Hunger for the city's deep, tired breath.
Footsteps
    Fall on paving stones.
Hardness.

Hunger, here.
    Here doesn't exist.
There,
    where breath and footsteps
    Move across rooftops.
There,
    in the non-existent distance,
    through the thin light of a fading dusk
    a woman arrives by train from beyond the known.

The third draft began when Horak returned from treatment. This was a big draft, the push from the still raw second to the mostly polished and finished third. This push almost ruined both of us. We worked intensely, inhumanely. Horak, as expected, quickly fell off the wagon again, though this was a necessary precondition for success. An only sober Horak was half a Horak, after all. The drinking escalated. Alena couldn't even successfully intervene with him and eventually got sick of me calling her in the middle of the night to attend to him. "Don't call me unless he's close to dead," she shouted at me one night, though sadly these instructions still necessitated at least one call per week. But all the suffering was worth it. The third draft pushed the novel to the edge of completion. Carrying it over that edge would take five more excruciating years. Perhaps without this trip back to Maine the end would never have happened. Maine. Gabe. Ida. I returned to Prague after my trip very near mental collapse and faced a stark choice, which I presented to Horak in an incredible verbal brawl some weeks ago. My options, I shouted at him, were one of the following: a) I could check myself into a mental hospital; b) I could commit suicide; c) we could finish the book as quickly as possible without any delay. Even though I'm not a suicidal type, I felt at the end, exhausted, lost, confused and broken. I felt that Horak had checkmated me. He must have sensed that this desperation was no superficial performance. "Okay," he said, "we finish it, Sy. We finish. We finish."

But Pepi—I lost sight of her. Pepi got crushed by the movement from the second to the third draft. I would've probably had a great life with Pepi. I loved her, maybe even more than I ever thought I loved Ida. But it didn't happen. It couldn't happen. A couple of years ago, as Horak and I were taking a break from the revision, I stepped out on his balcony and looked down over the park. There she was, Pepi, pushing a stroller with a light green top. She was with a guy—tall, lean, and unshaven. It was Ivan Novak, another poet from the Prague scene. My stomach churned. I hated Novak at that moment (and still). He got what I failed to get. He got a life, a future! I remember that day with total clarity. I went back inside and saw that Horak had fallen asleep in his chair, beer in hand. A thin stream of drool issued from his mouth and was trickling onto his shirt just below the breast pocket. There was already a stain from the drool about the size of my palm. Disgusting. Disgusting Horak, beautiful Horak!

"I have to confess something," Claire said as she broke into this bitter moment of reflection.

"What's that?"

"I don't know *Rain, Rain.*"

"Then why did you say you've read it?"

"I don't really know. It felt like the thing to say at the time. Maybe it would've been even better if I'd been reading it at that very moment, right here at the bar. Too unbelievable, I guess."

"I guess so," I said, too inebriated by now to follow these twists and turns. I had no clue what to make of this frivolous mendacity.

"Sorry to say, but I really need to get going. Snow or not, it's time for me to lie down. I'm not a drinker. Two is usually my limit and now I've lost count of how many drinks I've had."

"I understand."

"Are you staying in the hotel?"

"My plan is to make it to my brother's house north of here, but if that's not possible I might curl up in a corner of the lobby upstairs. Or underneath this table and hope nobody notices me."

"There's plenty of room in 401. Far too much for just me."

She got up and slung her bag over her shoulder. I saw the tip of that paperback book sticking out of the top and wondered again what she'd been reading at her place at the bar, reading with such focus and intensity, and at the same time distractedly, fearfully. I wondered if it could possibly have been *Rain, Rain*, even without her knowing. Gabe was outside in the snow with Elsie. He'd come back, I thought, and we'd journey to that frontier, somewhere beyond civilization, beyond Claire, beyond Elsie.

"Tell them I said goodbye," she said as she pushed in her chair.

"Sure," I said, "if they ever come back. But how can I reach you again?"

"You can knock on the door of room 401."

That was it. Claire was gone. She ascended back into the land of the living. She passed through that marble-floored lobby on the way to the elevator and then down the hall to the door where she'd fumble with the key, enter the room, kick off her shoes and collapse on the bed without changing her clothes. Living—up there people were living, moving back and forth with purpose. They entered the lobby from outside, took off their winter coats and shook the snow to the floor. I took a deep breath, now accustomed to the bar's stale air. Two guys had just given up their positions at the bar, so I moved over there and sat back down on a stool, putting my jacket over the adjacent one to hold it for Gabe and my suitcase beside my feet. It was convenient, I thought, that there was no stool for Elsie. It was time to move beyond whatever it was Gabe and I hadn't moved beyond earlier in the evening.

I sat drinking my beer and thinking of room 401. It was a good, clear offer and would, in any case, save me the $40 it would cost to hire a cab to take me to Henry's place in Freeport, that is, if any taxi would even agree to drive me in such weather. Maybe, it occurred to me, I had appealed to Henry and not to my father for that money to see me through the Horak project. Maybe it was Henry all along who told me that there would never be an end to

166

it. Now look at me! Look! I'm sitting by pale lamplight at my antique walnut-wood desk, which a balding and bespectacled clerk had assured me once belonged to Karl Entz-Kinzelberger, first cousin to Rainer Maria Rilke. I'm looking out at the empty narrow street below my apartment and it is finished. Or basically finished. It will be finished tomorrow when I get those last pages initialed. Tomorrow—or, more precisely, later today, as the hour now approaches 4am. Horak will scrawl those final initials JLH, and then I'll rush the thing to the post office and mail it express delivery to the Chief in New York, sending him a message as soon as my feet hit the sidewalk in front of Horak's apartment—it's done! And without needing to receive the parcel, the Chief's machine will set in motion and the wheel of history will turn and *Blue, Red, Gray* will be a reality. An hour together, possibly two, that's all we'll need. I'll read the pages to Horak as he starts his first beer of the day around 11am. He'll close his eyes and listen. Perhaps once or twice something will irritate him and he'll flare up. We might argue. He might curse. He might throw his bottle of beer against the wall. But in the end, he'll settle back into the armchair and we'll continue. He'll sip his Pilsner and again shut his eyes and drift into those elusive and mysterious thoughts. Yes, I will get those initials on each page. And then I'll quietly leave and quietly shut the door behind me. And Horak will be gone. Horak will in that very instant disappear from my life. I'll finally be free of him and he from me.

I don't remember whether it was Henry or my father who sent me those traveler's checks. I can't even remember now exactly when it was that my father locked himself in his office with my grandfather's old typewriter (a 1930s Remington) or whether it was before or after they tried to push him out of his job. Was it Henry who told me that I'd never be finished with Horak, that Horak had no end? To have no end, for Henry, meant failure—and to end something was the mark of its success. All acts require completion, the completion defines it. An incomplete act, a partial act, a push toward the infinite—this was, for Henry, nothing but folly or madness. Folly, yes, Horak was folly. And *Blue, Red, Gray* was madness. Only idealists or Utopian dreamers imagined endless things. The Berlin Wall fell. That was an end, right? Havel went to Prague Castle. And tomorrow—today—only hours from now—I will get my end. Horak will be complete and then disappear from my life. And then? And then? And then?

Gabe came in and removed his hat and jacket. From my perspective at the bar, he looked to be in a strange state of mind. His olive color seemed drawn and pale. His hair, after the hat removal, was a rumpled mess. He seemed surprised—and not pleasantly so—to see me back at the bar alone. I don't think he was ready for it. I wasn't either.

"Where's Elsie?"

"She took off to look for Paul."

"I didn't know you smoked."

"I don't," he said and then called over to Chuck. "Another round over here."

Silence. Silence stretched for a tense minute or two. We had to get there, to get back there. There was no other direction for us but back. He turned and looked at me without saying anything. It was the same look he'd given me after I finished my description of *Blue, Red, Gray*.

"Has Ida ever been this way before?"

He continued to stare at me, unblinking. I could see the tiny reflections of myself on his glassy eyes. "After she got back from Berlin. For a few months—maybe half a year."

"What did she say about it? About Berlin?"

"Nothing much. Some things. Some things here and there and most of these much later. It was buried for a while. And then it started to surface, piece by piece, like an excavation."

"And you think this time is related to that?"

"I didn't think about it that way until your letter came. And now here you are. But did you ever leave, Sy? Did you ever really leave here?"

I don't know exactly what Gabe meant by this question, but for some reason I felt compelled to say, "No, I guess I didn't. I've been here the whole time."

"There's one part of the whole thing that I've never understood. Why did you take off to Prague? Why did you leave Berlin?"

"I got the job there, you know that. Horak was there."

"Or you got lost there," he said and then paused. "You ran away and lost yourself there."

"That's wrong."

"Henry told me he visited you about a year ago. He was distressed when he came back. I've never seen him like that."

"Henry's never stepped foot in Prague."

"Goddammit, Sy. What the hell's wrong with you? What the hell are you doing?"

"Ida said to come. Her letter said to come. Do you really want me to dig it out of my suitcase and read it to you? Will it come to that? Will we go as far as to read Ida's letter together in this place? This place, this horrible place of all places?" Gabe shook his head. I thought for a moment and then said, "The thing about Horak, despite his huge

170

personal flaws, maybe in some sense precisely because of them, he's able to rise. He rises above history. He drags history forward."

"Nobody rises out of history. History's nothing that can be dragged. It's nothing. It's an invention."

"You're wrong, Gabe. Just because you've decided to stay here and float slowly down the river doesn't mean that things aren't moving and churning around you. You've stowed your paddle while Horak stands at the mouth of the river and tries to change its course, to reverse its flow away from the ocean, to make the river climb its mountain. He does this by the power of his will and genius."

"And where are you on this river?"

"Where am I? Isn't it obvious? I'm in Horak's massive shadow, Gabe. I am his shadow."

"Or he's yours."

"That's physically impossible. The sun is setting on Horak. It casts his shadow far behind him. It stretches toward the horizon."

"Enough of shadows," Gabe said and turned back to his beer. His eyes were cast down at the marble surface of the bar. "I've had all I can take of shadows."

"Is she waiting for you outside?"

"Who?"

"Elsie."

"I told you, she went to look for Paul."

"But I doubt Paul can be found."

"There's no way of knowing."

"Do you remember the book of Job, Gabe? I go East and He's not there, West and do not perceive Him, North and He's concealed, South and He is hidden. I do not see Him. I cried out to You, but You did not answer me. I hoped for light, but darkness came."

"What's the point?"

"What do you believe, Gabe? What do you believe in?"

"I'm not thinking much about belief these days. Are you pretending to be Job? That's taking it way too far, Sy. If you're Job, it's because you've chosen to be Job, which means you're no Job at all."

"Have you ever asked Ida what she believes in?"

"What's that supposed to mean? Be very careful here."

"There's no way for me to be careful now. Forget that, forget careful. What about it? Have you asked her? Have you ever once said, Ida what do you believe in? Tell me. Tell me that."

"I don't need to ask her a question like that. When you know someone like I know Ida, you know. You understand."

"That's a mistake, Gabe. I asked her once. I asked her on one of those dark winter nights."

"So tell me, Sy, enlighten me. What does Ida believe in?"

"She believes in what follows the sixth recession. I could tell you were sensing it when I talked about Mondschein and Kostel and that scene in the chapel. I could see it in your eyes when I mentioned Day Seven. Ida believes in Day Seven, Gabe. She longs for total reconciliation, for putting back what's broken."

He stood up abruptly from his stool, moved his face close to mine and said in a sort of whisper-shouting voice, "Don't be a fool."

I was pretty drunk, not overwhelmingly drunk, but drunk. I was tired from the long trip. It had been well over twenty-four hours since I'd last slept. The night before I left, I'd had a session full of torment with Horak, which didn't come to an end until nearly dawn.

"You're the fool," I shouted as I rose to my feet to look him in the eye, "the pathetic fool who sits down here in this forgotten place—this nowhere place—because you're too scared to imagine how different things could be. That's what's always been missing, Gabe. You end at the beginning. All your ends are beginnings. But you can't see it. You can't even sense it. I might not be able to end *Blue, Red, Gray*, but that's because it has no end. As long as Horak has breath, the book doesn't end. But Horak is fading

173

away. That's right, he's fading into oblivion. And then it'll be over. The Chief will have his prize. Millions of dollars will be made and the author and the translator won't get a penny. And anyone who knows the reality of things will see that this end won't be a celebration. It'll be a tragedy, because this fading into oblivion means the extinguishing of a long-burning flame of creative genius. It'll point to the mortality of genius. Think about the line from *Snowfall*—the sister says it, more to herself than to her brother. She says, 'There's nothing more unsettling than when the snow stops falling.' That was the only real line you've ever written. You don't even know how close you were to the truth."

Gabe sat back down on the stool and tried to gather himself. I did the same. Apparently, we had been making quite a bit of commotion and by now nearly everyone in the bar was staring at us. I felt the urge to get out of there. My whole body seemed to be pressing me to get up and bolt for the door—to the fresh air, to the fresh snow. I'd call Henry from somewhere and he'd jump into his car and come rescue me from the storm. It wouldn't be the first time.

"I was fourteen years old when I met Ida," Gabe said. Needless to say, I knew this well enough. "It feels like we've spent lifetimes together."

174

"You never told me that summer that you were writing for Ida. You were concealing it from me."

"I was writing for myself. In the first version, the first draft, the character was a young man, a boy—and I was going to act in it. But at some point I realized it wasn't right. It had to be a girl and that girl had to be Ida. That's when it started to come together. That's what made it work."

"Then the girl who's preparing to give the eulogy was originally you?"

"A boy. Yes. And it wasn't a eulogy for his brother. It was for his friend. His best friend. For you, Sy."

"So you wanted to get rid of me already then, to kill me off. But isn't that what you ended up doing?"

"No, I wanted to bring you back. Don't you get that? I always wanted to bring you back."

"I don't believe it. I don't believe anything you're saying to me now. I want you to tell me why you asked me to meet you in this place. I want to know why I'm sitting here."

I must have been shouting again, because as soon as I said this I felt a hand on my shoulder.

"Hey, Kirschbaum, settle down." It was Morgan. "The guys and me are starting to think there'll be more blood spilled here tonight than on the ice in Buffalo. And that would be saying a lot, considering the boxing match we just witnessed."

"I'm fine," I said, "I'm fine."

"If you say so. Are you sure?"

"Yes."

"Either of you need a lift?" Morgan said, looking over at Gabe to assess, I guess, what he was thinking.

We both shook our heads.

"Okay, then, if you say so. The boys and I are heading out. Can't push it too far. We're getting old, not young like you guys. Have to get up for work tomorrow."

I was about to let him go with just a nod, but then felt a rush of energy. "Let me ask you a question, Morgan. What is it you like about hockey?"

Morgan seemed taken aback by the inquiry.

"Why I like hockey?"

"Yes, what is it that compels you to sit there in front of the screen? What makes you feel something for this sport? I've been trying to understand this for years."

"It's a beautiful game."

"I don't find it beautiful at all. I find it hideous and ridiculous. All those guys dressed like medieval knights on skates, zipping around on ice and banging a small rubber object with sticks. Colliding with each other, crashing into the wooden sides. Smashing each other. Fighting."

"Come on, Kirschbaum, give it a break. Sure, the violence is one thing. But there's also the gracefulness. The skills those guys have in handling the puck is incredible. The speed that they move, awesome. The subtlety of the positioning and strategy. This is athleticism at its best. You can't help but admire it. But it's not an intellectual thing, Kirschbaum, it's physical. Pure physicality. You need to let go and enjoy the physicality of hockey. That's something I'm pretty sure your brother understands. He was a stout defender in his day. I can remember some fine moments in his high school career. Man, could he hit. He had a pretty decent slap shot, too. Don't get me wrong when I say this, Kirschbaum, but I think—I mean, I'm pretty darn sure— that what you find ridiculous about hockey is only what you find wanting in yourself."

Physicality. Flesh. Movement. Collision. Exertion. Words tumbled around in my mind, some coming close to spilling out of my mouth in no particular order and with no particular meaning. Instead, I sensed that issuing from my lips was a faint whistling sound, like wind through the crack in a windowpane. What did Morgan take me for—a monk? I was no stranger to the realm of the flesh. And yet I couldn't quite bring myself to refute him. A line from Mondschein, from the famous Rodrigan commentary on the covenant of the circumcision, said something like that those who forget the flesh and imag-

177

ine themselves as an idea, as only an idea, will become tyrannical or insane.

"Seriously, Kirschbaum, tell your brother to give me a call. And get home safe."

With that, Morgan patted me on the shoulder, shook hands with Gabe, and left the bar after his friends. At the moment he disappeared into the darkness of the stairwell, I felt sorry to see him go.

Then I realized, apart from anything to do with hockey, that Gabe's one-act in high school was actually the first draft of his masterpiece *Snowfall.* Yes, the brother and sister in *Snowfall* were the brother and sister of the earlier work, here the brother brought back to life. In *Rehearsal for a Eulogy,* he is gone. But isn't he, I thought, basically gone in *Snowfall,* too? He's taken a first step out of life. Lustful—Elsie had got it just right. I wanted her to return to the bar and to sum it up for us as only she could do, as only her "lustful" could do. I turned and again saw Paul's jacket hanging there. It meant a return. It demanded a return. Or it signified abandonment, giving up, a sacrifice. She had eyes like Ida's eyes. She had Ida's mouth and Ida's neck and Ida's thin, delicate fingers.

The nights fold together like two pages facing each other in a book, the ink still wet from the printing. There's no use worrying about smudges and the transfer of letters and words from one side to the next. My apartment in Prague transforms into that musty bar. Recollection and event merge and become indistinguishable.

"And *Snowfall,* is that also about us, about two friends?"

"Maybe it is."

"Are we brothers, Gabe?"

"I don't know."

"There's a theory that Cain kills Abel out of jealousy for a woman. Do you think all violence, all hate, can be boiled down to that?"

"I don't know that theory, Sy, but there's no murder in the play. And I don't give a damn about Cain or Abel."

"Who's Cain here, Gabe? You or me?"

"No one's Cain. And no one's Abel. There are no archetypes. We're all too damn human."

"Ida Fields is an archetype. You conjured her. She stepped right out of your imagination and onto the Deering High School stage. And she became flesh. And then she vanished after the final performance. Poof. Gone. She'd played her role. She'd eulogized the dead. She'd made sense of the loss and the book of life was closed and sealed. It was over then and there, Gabe. Over. You have to accept it. You have to let it go."

"Another round, Chuck," Gabe called out.

"I'm sure you don't want to hear this, Gabe, but I'm going to tell you a memory from those months with Ida in Berlin. I know it'll sting. There's nothing I can do about that. It'll sting like hell. It was late February or early March. Doesn't really matter. The important thing is that there was a spell of warm weather that brought something of a premature flowering of springtime to the city. It was after midnight and Ida and I took bikes and rode down to the river to find a squat where a friend of mine was organizing some late night events. But we never made it there—couldn't find the building amid the row of gutted, crumbling structures. After awhile, we decided to park the bikes and try our luck on foot, heading into the ruins. From one such structure, we heard faint sounds of music coming from somewhere within. It was impossible to tell where it was coming from. The dark mass of brick loomed overhead. We found a staircase and climbed to the top floor. Walls, which were crumbling away, only partially encased the rooms. All the glass from the windows had been broken and removed and now the warm, balmy air filled the space. The remains of the walls were covered by one layer of graffiti over another. Generations of graffiti, dating back to the 1960s, perhaps all the way back to the Russian invasion in 1945. The back of the building overlooked the Spree. We made our way there and looked down at the lights reflecting in the dark water. There was no sign of anyone. No traces that anyone called this space his home—however temporarily. We continued from one room to the next. All the same condition, graffiti, the windows gaping holes, the old parquet floors scratched and beaten but still elegant, the high ceilings with their ornate moldings reflecting an earlier grandeur. As we made a final turn into the last room facing the river, we saw that the façade had completely fallen away. It was unclear how the roof remained propped up overhead. But this huge opening allowed the moonlight to completely fill the space and all of a sudden it seemed like we were standing in silvery daylight. Then I turned and saw on the wall opposite an unforgettable sight. This was no ordinary piece of graffiti, Gabe. No. This was as pure a work of art as you could ever imagine. A wild burst of rapture amid the ruins. Ida came up behind me as I moved toward it, pulled in by its incredible perfection. She put her arms around me as I reached out and pressed the palm of my hand against it. It felt both cold and alive—like it contained some hidden electric pulse still coursing through the deadened brickwork. You know what happened then, Gabe, what happened there. I took her and pressed her to that work of art. And she blended into it. She became it. And then from inside that wall she reached out and pulled and pulled until I entered the work of art, too."

"Enough, enough!" Gabe shouted. "What are you doing? There's absolutely no point to this."

"There's actually a big point. I'm trying to tell you where Ida is, Gabe. She's in there. In that wall. In that color. She never came out again. She's in that moonlit blue and red and gray." Gabe was staring straight ahead. He didn't look good. He looked downright horrible. "That's where she is," I repeated, having found that after uttering this phrase, I couldn't let it go. "That's where she is."

He took a drink and then wiped his mouth with his sleeve.

"I think it's time to call Henry," he said.

"I can't do that now. I came to see Ida. I came because of that letter."

"That letter," he started and then paused. He thought for a second and took another drink. He seemed to be bracing himself. "Okay, Sy, let's agree to have one more beer and then call it a night. We'll talk again tomorrow. I'll call you at Henry's in the afternoon."

"If Ida doesn't sleep, as you say, it would be better to see her now."

"That's not possible. You know that. You know very well that that's never going to happen."

"Because you're blocking it. As I suspected, that's the whole point of this meeting. No cell phone reception. That's pure theater. And a lie."

"I'm not blocking anything."

Twenty-five years after the fall of the Berlin Wall and the Velvet Revolution. Chaos, years of chaos, years of clarity vanishing into the fog of relativism, into the same forest where Kostel disappeared at the edge of dusk. Yes, the wall fell and the empire crumbled and the only thing we could say for sure—this is evil—fades into a colorless moral sameness, all color tending toward the gray. And now Gabe claims that he's not blocking anything and that I hopped on the plane and that he doesn't know the meaning of that letter, robbing Ida of both voice and body. I came here for her.

"In any case, let's have one more drink," I said.

"Good," he said and signaled to Chuck. "Fine."

We sat there in silence for a while. The bar was finally starting to clear out. It seemed that Claire's departure had led the way. To room 401—the space contains all my desires, a space high above me in some inaccessible domain. It's true, I thought, I could knock on that door, if such a door exists on such a hall. As I considered this, I had the distinct impression that the hotel had no fourth floor and thus 401 would be a room without floors, walls or ceiling.

And what was a room without any quality of roomness, without dimensions, without objects like a bed or chair or mirror or carpet or television set? Where would desire find its fruition in such a room as this? Yes, perhaps our bodies could float in the darkness as snow fell over us, covering us in fine white powder, mixing its coldness with our heat, its verticality with our horizontality, its ice with our fire. 401. Perhaps, I thought, warm air would blow in from the south and turn the snow to rain. Everything newly buried would emerge.

"Elsie reminds of Ida. I thought it immediately. You can't deny it—a young Ida Fields. The only Ida I knew. She has Ida's passion. And that passion might be the whole thing. If you remove that, you remove what's essentially Ida about Ida. What remains, then?"

"You can't remove it."

"Maybe it's been transformed. Or transferred from Ida to her. It floated out of one body and into another."

"There's no replicating Ida. No way. She's too damn singular. What's the point of thinking about things that way? Elsie's got her own thing. She doesn't need to be Ida."

"Are you in love with her?"

"Of course not."

"But you will be. After she nails that lustful monologue. It'll be impossible not to fall in love with her, with youth, beauty, spirit, and the promise of a future."

"I'm not giving up on Ida. I'm nowhere near that. She's still right there in the guestroom. She's sitting up in bed with her grandmother's old quilt spread out over her legs. And Hannah's still asking when she's coming out, when she's getting up, if she's awake yet. I'll never give up on her. She's all I've got. All the rest can go to hell. I'm not looking for anything beyond that. I'm done looking."

"What are you going to do?"

"I'm going to go back to the beginning. I need to find my way back there."

"To Ida alone on stage, dressed in her white silken robe, and lit up by that luminous spotlight."

"To that first time I saw her."

"And you think that's possible?"

"I have no choice."

"What about all those intervening years between then and now, what do they amount to?"

"A split second. That's it."

"She was perfect in the play, Gabe."

"She was, she made it—she brought it to life."

I looked over at Paul's jacket hanging there. It was a vintage-looking brown leather jacket with a thick woolen

185

lining. Something about that jacket just hanging there reminded me of a meeting I'd had with Horak's daughter some days before I left Prague for my trip to Maine. Before this meeting, it'd been a year or more since I'd seen her. We met because she said she wanted to discuss the end stage of the translation. The setting was the Café Savoy on the other side of the river from my apartment, a beautiful but hardly bearable place, whose aesthetically perfect cakes were always way too dry. The coffee was no better. But what did I really care about dry cake or harsh, thin coffee? After we'd ordered, Anna told me that she'd heard that Carl Glaser had "greenlighted" (she actually used that Englishism even though we spoke in Czech) me to write a translator's preface to the forthcoming first printing of *Blue, Red, Gray*. I confirmed this and told her not to worry, that I'd already brought together my notes and that the preface would in no way delay publication. Her face grew quite stern as I said this. She told me that she'd recently reviewed the 1997 contract and could find nothing in it that mentioned a translator's preface. You're right, I said, but it had been years since the issue had been discussed and settled on. And in any case, I added, the reader of such a massive and historically significant work expected to hear from the translator. Horak had also agreed. She turned away from me and gazed out the window as a red and white streetcar rumbled by. That might have been true in the past, she said, but it wasn't the case any longer. Then she said the unimaginable: "Horak doesn't trust you." Doesn't trust me! This was nonsense. I didn't believe it—and still don't believe it. There was nobody, including Anna, whom Horak trusted more than me! The reality was that Anna had prevailed against me and was now settling old scores. But what did the reason matter? My preface would not appear in the book. I had been banished from the text, my text.

I stood up and as calmly as I could (my whole body was shaking), placed my napkin on the table, took out five hundred crowns from my wallet, and dropped it down beside my half-eaten piece of Sachertorte. Then I left the Café Savoy. It took half a dozen shots of whiskey at a bar a few blocks away to steady my nerves.

Gabe spoke, interrupting my memory. "We've got a piece of land up north. It's about fifteen acres, maybe a little more. I bought it after college when we decided to stick around here. I got the land cheap. It's off of an old logging road near Rangeley. At first, I didn't have any plans for it. Ida and I would head up there a few times a year, walk through it, and try to get a sense of the land. I'd try to imagine what we might build there someday. We'd set up a tent and cook some food over a fire. It's incredible how little artificial light is up there, how big the sky seems when you climb Moosehead Peak to the west. Huge. Wide open. It's as open as I can imagine the world could ever be; it's as clear a vision as I'll ever be privileged to see. Then as soon as the car door shuts for the ride back it all closes down. After a while, Ida stopped coming. I can't remember precisely when. It didn't seem to mean much at the time. I'd still go, though not as often as before, especially after Hannah was born. I usually went a few times a year, once in June, again in August or September, maybe once in winter. I'd walk, note down some things, and make a sort of map of the terrain. Amazing how you can get to know a piece of land like that. It's like knowing a body, its undulations, scars, scents, and its past. At the same time, the land has no past. Not that it's virgin soil, nothing like that, but it's still as close as I've ever come to purity. To exist in such a place for any length of time shifts your balance. And then when you return from up there you feel the balance gradually move back, even if you don't want it to. At some point, I got the inspiration to build a cabin there. I planned to do it by myself with my own two hands. Ida liked the idea and we thought that eventually we'd give up our apartment here and move up there. It took a while to identify and clear the right area for the foundation. But once that was done, once the clearing had been made, I hesitated. I couldn't imagine what the next step would be. I'd dreamed up dozens of potential plans but couldn't commit to any of them. Last summer, Hannah came up with me for the first time. We stayed for three nights, set up a tent in the middle of that same clearing, now overgrown with weeds and saplings. It was intense for her. She talked constantly about Ida, wanted to know what Ida had thought of this and that. I could tell she wanted to feel her there. In the end, in one way or another it was just too much wilderness for her, and maybe for Ida, too. Not for me. For me, it's a sanctuary. You take deep breaths, one after another, a breath, a release, a breath. You can actually learn to breathe up there. It's hard to describe. All I know is that it's a totally different way of breathing than we do down here. Down here we breathe in reaction to things. You hold your breath in the chest for one or two or three seconds too long without letting it go at the right time. This delay throws everything else off. Build, plant, hike, and observe—just being aware of what's happening around you. That's what it's about up there. You asked me what Ida believes in. She believed in what I believed, what I still believe—that everything imaginable is contained within those fifteen acres. Everything imaginable and everything possible, the entire universe, is there. But she lost that faith. Now she's stranded."

At the very moment Gabe fell silent, a couple of people rose from their stools, put on their jackets and headed for the staircase that led up to the hotel lobby, opposite the stairs through which I had descended to the bar. I looked over to that other staircase in hopes that maybe Elsie or Paul would be back again. Nothing. Nothing! For god's sake, I should stop the whole thing right here before I really lose my nerve. It must be close to dawn by now and my hand is starting to shake. It was already well past midnight on that night with Gabe in Maine and I should have called it quits then, too, or truthfully well before. I should have stopped this story a few notebook pages back before Gabe told me about that land. This was much more than I could take—can take! I should have put down my mechanical pencil after Ida had vanished into that moonlit wall of color. Or I should have ended the whole thing with those three months in 1997 beginning in the Tempelhof Airport and ending on that platform at Zoo Station as I boarded the train for Prague. On the other hand, there was no way to end there. God knows I have trouble identifying the precise point at which the curtain should fall. This was Gabe's domain and Gabe kept on writing, wrote his way to that land and back again and again and again in endless circles of Junes and Septembers and winters. To the land and its cabin, which only existed in his imagination, an imaginary cabin from which Ida had fled in horror. Horak, too, was no ender of things. Unlike me, though, Horak transcended narration, flew above mundane, limited concepts like beginnings and endings and characters and narrative arc. And he didn't begin and end and he had no characters or story or climax or arc. He had only Totality. He had a mountain.

The land—it was clear that we needed to be there as soon as possible. "Let's drive to the land tonight. Let's go there now, Gabe. You have a car, right? That's the only possibility for us."

"It's the middle of the night and there's a blizzard out there."

"The snow's nothing. The darkness is nothing. I'm barely feeling tired anymore even though I've been up for days. Just the thought of stepping on that land has sent a jolt through me, a real jolt. We'll pick up some black coffee on the way. Black coffee's just the thing for us. We'll be there before dawn. Day will break wide open just as you described it. That's exactly what we need, to see a day breaking like that, to be done with this endless night. Day will break, tomorrow will be here, the snow will pass, the clouds will blow out to sea, and we'll climb Moosehead Peak and gaze into the distance." I got up off my stool as

I said this. Once the idea had its grip on me, I knew it wouldn't let me go.

"Sit down, Sy. It's not going to happen."

"Because of the storm? It's barely anything."

"It's wild out there."

"It doesn't matter. It could be the worst storm of the decade and it wouldn't matter to me at all. Just like the rainstorm that overtook Horak as he made his way to Sněžka. Some journeys transcend the physical. That's what Horak found out in the Chapel of Saint Lawrence. He met his demon there. Not his demon in any fabulist sense. I mean the exact person he was bound to meet, whom he needed to meet and to overcome if his book were going to make it to the West. That man was the regime, Gabe, the whole system in one body, one flesh. And Horak overcame him, as Jacob overcame God by fighting Him to a draw. But this overcoming, this conquering, was also the beginning of his end, his drinking, his escape, and his fading away step-by-step into irrelevancy. Worse. He lives now in a desert of creativity. Nothing more came to him or will ever come to him. His gift was bound by bigger forces, by structures he couldn't see or understand. He worked inside them, mastered them unwittingly and then killed what made him live. Now he fades away, every day a little less of him is there. What will happen to his shadow?

What happens to a shadow when its object of projection is gone? We need to go to the land, Gabe. We go tonight!"

"Just sit down, Sy. Sit down for god's sake and finish your beer."

"Haven't we had enough?'

"We'll have one more. It's last call, Chuck just announced it."

"One more and then we drive!"

"Just sit down. Sit. Chuck, two more beers over here."

I sat. My mind burned. My head spun. The vision of dense, snow-covered pines whipping by the sides of the road and illuminated by a pair of headlights pushed everything else from my sight. That was the forest's edge, I thought, the edge of existence—precisely that razor-thin edge over which Kostel passed beyond consciousness and into the tattered fabric of memory. Horak would soon follow. The book would be off to the Chief and with that the edge would be reached, an edge already traced long ago. The Chief had the page proofs ready. The cover had already been designed: a grainy photograph of a figure captured from behind as he stands atop Petřín hill and stretches his arms out toward Prague, the city veiled in a misty gray. I'd seen a mock-up of the book months before my trip to Maine. There would be no further changes, despite what happened in the initialing process. Horak had no will to alter anything anymore. With this, his book will reach the wider world. It's the first and only translation. The others in French, German, Russian and so on had long since failed. Anna had prevailed against me. There would be no note on the translation. As a consolation, the Chief offered me the chance to dedicate the book to someone. But who could this be? Who could represent these decades of labor, my youth lost, my mind and body rent and ruined? Ida Fields. As I wrote in my letter to her, "This book belongs to you." Horak, mercifully, agreed. There would be no book without Ida, he said, without the catalytic force that took me on a three-month and seventeen-year journey from Tempelhof Airport to Zoo Station, two spaces now lost in the past. An arrival at Tempelhof, a departure at Zoo. I wrote, *Dear Ida, this book belongs to you.* The Chief had it typeset. The page proofs contain the line. And then a call came from my old friend Gabe Slatky to meet him in that bar.

The last beers of the night arrived in front of us. In synchronized fashion, as if we were one and the same man, we finished our old beers, pushed the empty glasses away, took up the new ones, and sipped.

"She's not coming back, Gabe. Neither of them is coming back down here. Paul's jacket is going to hang there until Chuck or someone else comes and throws it into the lost and found. There's no sense waiting anymore. Finish your beer and we go north to the mountains. For us, the sun's been up for hours. It's noontime on the clearest summer day. Moosehead Peak beckons above us."

"It's time to call Henry. It's time, Sy. Let's go outside where my phone gets reception."

"No, we'll head north to the land near Rangeley. You'll show me that clearing and I'll imagine a cabin there."

"I need to be here for Hannah in the morning."

"Let Ida manage."

Gabe shook his head. "It's time to call Henry," he repeated. "There'll be no trip to the land."

"Then why did you tell me about it and the cabin and the clearing? Why are we in this place, Gabe? Why have I returned here?"

"To end what should have been ended a long time ago. I need this to be over now. Ida needs an end."

"I don't accept that. I don't believe it for a second. Ida would never say anything like that. If she wanted an end, she would have written it to me in the letter."

"That's what she needs. Believe it. It's real."

"It's a delusion, your delusion. It has nothing to do with Ida Fields."

"Sy, listen to me. It's real. It's reality."

"You've lost your way, Gabe. We need to find what's up there near Rangeley. What have you left behind up there?"

"There's nothing left to discover. It's all been known for long enough."

"Ida's letter said the opposite."

"It's time to call Henry. The bar's about to close."

"Henry's not coming. He was never coming. He doesn't even know I'm here."

A booming voice cut through our talk. "Closing time!"

"You heard the man," Gabe said as he stood up and slipped on his jacket. "I'll meet you outside. I'll call Henry in the meantime. I've got his number."

Before I had the chance to respond, with his long runner's strides Gabe had made his way across the space and into the stairwell through which I had entered the bar in the early evening. I called out to Chuck to settle up, but he told me he'd already put everything on Gabe's tab. I stood up and gazed around the bar. The last patrons filed out in both directions. I leaned against the bar, closed my eyes and imagined myself back in Prague at my desk in my apartment preparing my papers for a final session with Horak. It would be nearing dawn, like it is now, and I would be reaching out every so often, as I'm doing, to run my fingertips over the voluminous manuscript, that mountain of text. Horak. This was as much his body as his actual body,

196

as much his flesh as his actual flesh. I opened my eyes again and saw that I was alone in the bar. Chuck had flicked a switch and now the space was completely illuminated by a harsh white light, a light clearly meant to drive away the last sitters as quickly as possible.

I put on my jacket, took up my suitcase and started for the exit. Slowly, shakily I climbed the staircase and pushed open the door. The moment I stepped outside the swirling blizzard consumed me. I couldn't see more than a few feet in any direction. I called out for Gabe. He didn't answer. There was only wind and silence.

Seth Rogoff was born in Portland, Maine in 1976. He has translated several works by Franz Kafka, including *The Castle* (2007). He is currently working on a collection of fictional lectures and a nonfiction book on the politics of dream interpretation. He has been a creative writing Fulbright Fellow in Berlin, where he lived for ten years. Since 2015, he has lived with his wife Jana and their two children in Prague.

Photo by Tomáš Železný